The Inquisition
and Other Stories

MICHAEL TABOR

ISBN: 978-0-9986778-3-5 (paperback)
ISBN: 978-0-9986778-4-2 (hardcover)
ISBN: 978-0-9986778-5-9 (eBook)

The Inquisition and Other Stories is a work of fiction. Names,
characters, places, and incidents are the product of the author's
imagination, as are the roles played by various historical figures.
Any resemblance to actual persons, living or dead, events,
or locales, is entirely coincidental. The author thanks Doug
Levy of Feast for the wine pairings given in Table Talk.

Printed in the United States of America

Cover and Interior design by 1106 Design

For family and friends, as always.

CONTENTS

CATHERINE LESCAULT

Soon after arriving in Paris in 1612, the eighteen-year-old Nicolas Poussin visits the studio of the renowned artist Frans Pourbus the Younger. There he meets a mysterious old painter called Frenhofer who claims to have been the sole pupil of the Flemish master, Jan Mabuse. Frenhofer gives the two artists a profound lecture on art and the creative process as he brilliantly reworks Pourbus's painting, "Mary of Egypt". Frenhofer also tells them about a painting of his mistress, Catherine Lescault, a woman of incomparable beauty, that he has been working on for ten years. Pourbus tells Frenhofer that Poussin would be willing to let him use his beautiful young model, Gillette, in return for letting them see the painting of Lescault. Gillette unwillingly agrees to participate in this arrangement to prove her love for Poussin. A few months later this transaction takes place, and after spending a few minutes behind closed doors with Gillette, Frenhofer allows Poussin and Pourbus to see his masterpiece. All they find is a canvas covered with an incoherent jumble of colors—the only discernable feature being a perfectly drawn foot in one corner of the canvas. After a heated exchange over the painting, Frenhofer tells Poussin and Pourbus to leave his studio. During the argument between the three men, Gillette slips away. When Pourbus returns to Frenhofer's studio the next day he learns that Frenhofer has burned all his paintings that night and died in the process.

That is where the story, as told by Balzac in "The Unknown Masterpiece", ends. But many questions remain: what was the significance of the perfectly drawn foot, what happened to Gillette, who was Catherine Lescault and, above all, who was Frenhofer? Fortunately, some recently discovered papers of Nicolas Poussin answer these questions.

I, Nicolas Poussin, wish to record for the sake of posterity certain events that occurred in my youth and the remarkable consequences thereof that I experienced many years later. The critical events in question concerned my meeting with the mad genius Frenhofer in the studio of Frans Pourbus the Younger in the year 1612. While the immediate drama that followed is probably known to many readers of these pages, it is what happened thereafter that I wish to record here.

After Frenhofer had thrown Master Pourbus and me out of his studio I went back to my lodgings on Rue de la Harpe in search of Gillette. I stayed up the whole night hoping she would come to me, but she did not. The next day I went to Master Pourbus's studio on the Rue des Grands-Augustins to see if he had any news of her, thinking that she might have sought refuge with him. It was then that I learned the shocking news of Frenhofer's death in a fire that he himself had set to destroy all his paintings. Nothing of his work or his other treasures had survived the blaze.

I spent the next few days searching all over Paris for Gillette. I was assisted in this endeavor by her cousin, an apprentice in the workshop of Monsieur Freminet. Like me, the young man had heard reports that Catherine Lescault had made a hasty departure from Paris due to an incident involving a nobleman. But of Gillette he was as ignorant as me. We came to the somber conclusion that she had been the victim of some hideous crime and her corpse disposed of in the Seine.

I was inconsolable and was sure that I was the one ultimately responsible for Gillette's death. Over the next few weeks I hid in my room and grieved over the loss of my beautiful Gillette and obsessed over Frenhofer, Catherine Lescault, and Frenhofer's incomprehensible portrait of her. I was sure Catherine had information that could cast some light on the whole affair, but she had left Paris for some unknown destination. Some speculated she had gone to England. I also obsessed about that perfectly drawn foot on Frenhofer's canvas. What did it mean? What was its significance? Did it encode some secret message? But, of course, the canvas no longer existed and no further investigation on that topic was possible.

I went back to see Master Pourbus. His manner seemed distant. He told me he was unwell, greatly upset by the loss of his friend, and that he needed to be left in peace—a wish

I could certainly understand. While I was in his studio I noticed that *Mary of Egypt* was missing. Master Pourbus told me that, for him, the painting was more Frenhofer's than his and he felt it only fitting to destroy it. That, too, I could understand.

The whole episode had come to a dead end. Frenhofer was dead, Gillette was dead, and Catherine Lescault had vanished without a trace. Paris, being the city that it is, was soon consumed by other scandals and for most people *l'affaire Frenhofer* was soon forgotten.

However, a few months later, I had a remarkable encounter with an elderly gentleman who had studied the lives of the old Flemish masters. He had in his possession a remarkable tome, *The Schilder-boeck,* a collection of artists' biographies written by the Flemish painter and historian, Karel van Mander. At the time, I was poorly educated in the history of art and welcomed the opportunity to talk to a scholar about Mabuse and his students. He patiently translated into French the biographies of Mabuse and certain other painters, such as Lucas van Leyden and Jan van Scorel, with whom Mabuse had associated. Those biographies revealed that Mabuse, despite his fame as an artist, was a most dissolute fellow. But more importantly, there was no record of him ever having had any students. In addition, van Mander could not identify with any certainty the years of either Mabuse's birth or death. I asked the old scholar if he would care to give an estimate of those dates. Based on the events described in the biographies we had just read he estimated that Mabuse had been born in the early or mid 1470's, and died in the early 1530's. Given that it was now 1612, this meant that Mabuse had been born the best part of 140 years ago. I then had a stunning realization. The way Frenhofer had told me and Master Pourbus about his time with Mabuse—the way he had bailed him out of drunken brawls and his participation in various events that were described in those biographies—implied that he, Frenhofer, was already a mature adult when he claimed to have been Mabuse's student. At most he was probably twenty years younger than Mabuse. But that was impossible! It would make Frenhofer approximately 120 years old! And nobody had ever lived to that age except, if one believed the Bible, Moses. And even if Frenhofer had been thirty years younger than Mabuse, he would still be impossibly old.

It was now clear that Frenhofer, genius that he might have been, was a fraud. And given the way that Master Pourbus had supported his tales made me suspect that he, too, was part of that deception. I said nothing of this to the old gentleman and thanked him for his help. I then asked him to pose for me briefly and drew his portrait. Much to his delight, I gave it to him as a token of my respect for his scholarship.

I immediately went to Master Pourbus's studio, full of questions and no little anger. Pourbus refused to see me and shouted through his closed door that he could tell me nothing, and that he never wanted to see me again. I was greatly hurt by his rejection. Indeed, I had even hoped at one point that he might have taken me on as his student.

It was the shock of that sudden rejection that finally closed the Frenhofer affair for me. I went on with my life, found other teachers, including Elle and Lallemand, and worked hard to improve my skills as a painter. Those early years in Paris were difficult. I think I can say that the highlight of that period was my friendship with Philippe de Champaigne who helped me find employment working alongside him decorating the Luxembourg Palace under the direction of Nicolas Duchesne. Philippe was the only person to whom I confided all the details of those dramatic events of 1612.

In 1624 I moved to Rome, and thanks to the patronage of Cardinal Barberini and Cavaliere Cassiano dal Pozzo—who became a dear friend—I was able to establish myself as an artist of some distinction. But all that is known and recorded elsewhere. And as for Frenhofer, Gillette, and Catherine Lescault, they were all forgotten, as was Master Pourbus who had died in 1622. I did not attend his funeral.

One day in October of 1640, Cassiano visited me in my studio. He told me that a certain Count S., a Portuguese nobleman residing in Rome, had requested a meeting with me. The Count was a connoisseur of the arts with a very fine private collection, and a man reputed to be of great wealth. The meeting was held at the Count's sumptuously furnished residence on Strada Giulia. He was most cordial and expressed admiration for my work in the most generous terms. He then proceeded to show me his private collection that included rare drawings by Michelangelo and Leonardo da Vinci, etchings by Durer, paintings by Raphael and Botticelli, a panel by Fra Angelico, and a number of paintings by Flemish masters. The Count's discussion of these works confirmed his reputation for artistic taste and knowledge of the highest order. He then said that there was a particular matter he wished to discuss with me. I had assumed he was going to offer me a commission so I was greatly surprised when he asked me if I had known the artist Frans Pourbus the Younger during my early years in Paris. Up until that moment, I had all but forgotten about him. The only person who knew about my relationship with Pourbus was my dear friend Philippe de Champaigne, and I knew he would never have betrayed my confidences.

Not wishing to disappoint my gracious host, I merely said that I had met Master Pourbus on only a few occasions but would be happy to share with him what I knew of his paintings based on his work as Marie de Medici's court painter. I had a feeling that the count detected some evasion in my answer but, nonetheless, he continued to address me in the most gracious terms and invited me to view his most recent acquisition. We proceeded to a small, unfurnished room. In its center stood a draped easel. The Count removed the drape and there I saw Pourbus's painting, *Mary of Egypt,* as transformed by Frenhofer. It was with the greatest difficulty that I was able to restrain a gasp of amazement. The count explained that he had purchased the painting on the promise of the seller that it was a genuine Pourbus, even though it did not have the artist's signature. Although the Count claimed considerable knowledge of the artist's work, and felt it to be genuine, he wished to hear my opinion of it.

Seeing that painting after so many years brought back a flood of memories of that life-changing day in Pourbus's studio when I had first met Frenhofer. I recalled the magical way in which Frenhofer had transformed Pourbus's painting into a sublime masterpiece while, at the same time, giving us his brilliant lecture on painting and the meaning of art—a lecture that deeply influenced my subsequent artistic development. But more than that, I recalled my beautiful Gillette whose love I had lost as a result of my association with Frenhofer.

Although my immediate instinct was to run out of the room and away from that diabolical picture, I could not insult my host by doing so. I took control of myself and gave my opinion of the painting. I felt it prudent to proceed cautiously and began by talking in general terms about the Flemish school of painting that Pourbus would have studied in the workshop of his grandfather, Pieter Pourbus. I discussed the work of the Flemish master, Mabuse, who had shown how to impart a degree of Italianate elegance and sculptural solidity to his figures. I ventured the opinion that, despite Mabuse's influence on the painting of his fellow countrymen, his figures tended to be stiff and wooden, and lacked the physical grace and anatomical accuracy that artists of our time had achieved. I was gratified to see that the Count agreed with my assessment.

I then went on to state, however, that the painting we were viewing had transcended those limitations and was far superior to any of Pourbus's other works that I was familiar with. As I went into the details of the picture, I felt as though Frenhofer himself had somehow taken control of me, and it was he who was now speaking through me in his own words. I stated that the figure of Mary had a living presence that made one feel one could walk around her. By contrast, so many of Pourbus's figures in his other paintings looked as though they had been glued to the canvas. This comment caused the Count to chuckle and nod his head in agreement. I then analyzed the way in which Mary's bosom had been painted: how the choice of colors and play of light gave one the feeling that blood was coursing through her breasts—an effect that was lacking in Pourbus's other paintings where, at best, breasts were as cold as marble, if not as dead as wood. The Count, clearly as much of a connoisseur of women as of painting, smiled knowingly at these observations. I then proceeded to discuss the composition as a whole, and echoing much of what I had learned from Frenhofer argued that the artist had achieved a perfect balance between *disegno* and color, and had imbued the whole composition with the sense of a living event. This was so different from the majority of Pourbus's other paintings—and those of many other artists of his ilk—where the scenes had the static quality of a theatrical tableau, albeit embellished with elaborate details of costume and jewelry. With sufficient technical training there was no shortage of artists who could *depict* a scene with some accuracy, but it took a true artist to *express* that scene—something Pourbus had managed to achieve in this painting. As to whether the painting was an authentic creation of the artist, I ventured the opinion that it was, even though I knew, in truth, that it was not. However, to tell the truth would have revealed dark secrets that would have triggered an avalanche of gossip and scandalmongering—a pursuit beloved by our idle patrons and fiercely jealous brotherhood of artists.

To justify my statement, false as it was, I felt it necessary to hold forth on the role of inspiration in the life of the artist. The exceptional brilliance of Pourbus's painting compared to his other works might, indeed, lead one to doubt its authenticity or, if nothing else, to ask why this particular work transcended his others. I stated that all artists, even those of the greatest distinction at the height of their artistic maturity and creativity, are not always able to maintain an output of uniform quality. Something, I confessed, that was true of my own work. Simply put, we will produce, from time to time and for various reasons, a work that is superior to our other paintings. And the reasons for that are manifold. The inspiring force could be as varied as the embrace of a new lover or the tragic loss of an old one; that is, some singular emotional perturbation that drives the muse within us to new heights. I could only conclude that Pourbus had experienced some unusual event that had affected him in a way that resulted in this brilliant unknown masterpiece of his.

Although exhausted by my lengthy discourse I was gratified by the Count's expressions of genuine appreciation for it. He said he agreed with my conclusion about the painting's authenticity and that its excellence had been driven by some extraordinary event in the life of the artist at the time of its creation. This being so, he had now decided to show it only to visitors of the most refined taste and superior artistic scholarship.

Our meeting ended on the most cordial terms and the Count expressed a desire to visit my studio and to continue our discussion of art and the creative process. However, as he escorted me to his door we had a brief exchange of such shattering import that I feel compelled to record it exactly as it occurred. Just as I was leaving, I said,

"My dear Count, might I be permitted to ask from whom you purchased the painting?"

"Of course," he said, "the purchase was a story in itself."

"How so?" I asked.

"The seller was a lady. Although past her bloom of youth she possessed the most refined and mature beauty, the like of which I have rarely seen. Indeed, she had a face worthy of a portrait by a great master such as yourself."

"And what was her name, may I ask?"

"She said her name was Catherine Lescault. She was on a brief visit to Rome and returned to Paris yesterday."

At that point, fortunately for me, the Count's attention was distracted by the approach of a servant. If he had not been so diverted, he would have seen me turn a deathly white and stagger as though stabbed in the heart.

I returned to my studio in a state of the greatest agitation and it took several drafts of strong spirit to calm my nerves. Everything that had just transpired was so fantastic and so absolutely impossible. Pourbus had sworn to me that he had destroyed *Mary of Egypt,* and Catherine Lescault had, according to all the reports, left Paris soon after Frenhofer's death, most likely settling in England. For a few minutes, I tried to comfort myself with the idea that I had just dreamed the whole meeting with Count S. However, I was soon disabused of this foolish idea by the arrival of a messenger from the Count with a note thanking me for my assessment of the Pourbus painting and, as a token of his appreciation, two flasks of a rare wine from his cellar. The least I could do was to reply in kind. I sent the Count a note expressing my gratitude for his hospitality and two small drawings I had recently made in the Borghese gardens. They were, I have to say, some of my finest work and I was sure he would be well pleased with such a gift from an artist of my reputation.

I became obsessed with resolving the mystery of Pourbus's painting. There was no doubt that the painting in the Count's possession was the very same one I had seen in Pourbus's studio, so he must have lied to me about destroying it. But why would he do so? And was the woman who had just sold the painting to the Count really Catherine Lescault? Or was she an imposter? And if so, why of all people would she pretend to be Catherine? And, whoever she was, how did the painting come to be in her possession?

My work was the one thing that kept me from losing my mind over these apparently unanswerable questions, and, above all, the resurfacing of my feelings of guilt and shame over my treatment of Gillette. I had many commissions to complete and, most recently, a new professional challenge. Soon after my meeting with the Count, I received a letter from de Noyers, Secretary of State to Louis XIII of France, inviting me, at the command of the King, to return to Paris to undertake decorations at Fountainebleau and the Palais du Louvre. The terms of the offer were extremely generous and included the use of a spacious and well-appointed apartment overlooking the Tuilleries Gardens. As much as I would have preferred to stay in Rome and away from the intrigues of the French court, it was an offer I could not refuse. Also, returning to Paris would give me the opportunity to renew my friendship with Philippe de Champaigne who was now enjoying much success, and the favor of Cardinal Richelieu. Phillipe was the one person in whom I could confide about my meeting with Count S. and all its extraordinary implications. Furthermore, Phillipe's standing and connections might enable us to finally track down Catherine Lescault.

I arrived in Paris in December 1640. I will not bother to record the details of my arrival other than to say that I was treated with the greatest civility and kindness by Monsieur de Noyer and Cardinal Richelieu, and then honored by an audience with the King. His Majesty was most gracious and did me the honor of appointing me his First Painter.

My greatest personal pleasure, however, was to be reunited with my old friend, Phillipe. He, too, was amazed by my account of the reappearance of *Mary of Egypt* and, in particular, the reappearance of Catherine Lescault. He undertook discreet inquiries on my behalf to find her. However, despite his connections at Court he could not find any news of her, and after a few months we gave up the search. I was so consumed by my heavy responsibilities as First Painter that I had all but forgotten about her until, out of the blue, a note was delivered to my apartment that said:

> *If you wish to meet Catherine Lescault, be at the front entrance of the Eglise St. Etienne-du-Mont at 5 o'clock tomorrow afternoon.*

On arriving at the church, I was approached by a boy who asked me to follow him to a nearby residence. There, a maid conducted me to a tastefully furnished study where I was asked to wait for a few minutes. I had just started to examine the books and decorations when I heard the sound of a door opening behind me. When I turned I saw a woman standing by the door. My artist's eye immediately discerned a perfectly formed figure clad in a beautifully tailored dress. But she was wearing a dark veil and I could not see her face. I bowed and said,

"Do I have the honor of addressing Madame Catherine Lescault?"

"No, Sir," she said, "you do not."

But before I could say another word, she lifted her veil. All I can remember was crying out "Gillette!" and then finding myself lying on a sofa with Gillette, still radiantly beautiful after so many years, smiling at me as she waved a vial of smelling salts under my nose.

"To think," she said with a laugh, "the great Nicholas Poussin, a Frenchman no less, fainting at the sight of a beautiful woman."

This is what Gillette told me. Some stories are so remarkable that they have to be true, since it would be impossible to make them up. She first told me what had transpired when she was alone with Frenhofer behind the closed doors of his studio.

Frenhofer told me to disrobe. He said he was not going to violate me in the sense he assumed I feared. I was too frightened to understand what he meant by that, let alone trust him to keep his word given the way he was ravishing

me with his eyes. The only thing that comforted me was hearing you shout through the door that you had drawn your dagger and would break the door down and kill him if he should hurt me. Frenhofer then got on his knees and took my right foot in his hands and proceeded to caress and kiss it in the most lascivious manner; an act that clearly gave him intense carnal satisfaction. If that was not enough—and what followed was truly revolting—he then sucked my toes like a depraved animal. Don't forget, I was only seventeen at the time and although I had experienced physical love, in its natural form with you, I was still ignorant of men's darker desires and perversions. He then got up and went to his canvas. With one hand he drew something and with the other…well, it should not be difficult for you to imagine what he did with it. He was an absolutely vile and disgusting old man.

He then told me to get dressed and showed me the canvas. It was covered in a formless mess of colors and, in one corner, the drawing he had just made—a drawing of my foot. Having heard so much from you about his ten-year effort to paint the beautiful Catherine Lescault—the painting you had asked me to sacrifice my honor for—I asked him where her portrait was. He told me that the painting did not exist, that she did not exist. That it was all a fiction to lure me into his studio to satisfy his desires. He also told me that Master Pourbus, who was deeply in his debt, knew all of this and was complicit in the deceit. The only person in the dark was my naïve young lover. An artist, he added, who was destined for greatness. It was then that he opened the studio door and invited you and Master Pourbus to view his canvas. While the two of you argued with Frenhofer, I slipped away—never to see you again until now. Why Frenhofer revealed his dark secrets to me, I do not know. Perhaps he assumed he had subjugated me into the silence of shame. How wrong he was.

Later that night I went back to his residence and threatened him with disgrace and ruin. I had recalled you telling me of his claim that he had been the pupil of a famous painter called Mabuse. Although I was ignorant of the arts I sensed that Frenhofer was a fraud and that this claim was false, even though I had no evidence to prove it. Nonetheless, I told him that I had incontrovertible proof that he had never been a pupil of Mabuse, or any other artist of note. Not only would I tell the world of his dishonesty, I would also let it be known that he was an impotent old fool who preyed on innocent young women to gratify his perverted desires. In addition to disgrace he would be the object of ridicule. And, furthermore, he would most likely end up being drowned in the Seine by my lover with the eager assistance of his friends. Frenhofer believed my threats and broke down. He confessed that he had never been a student of Mabuse, and begged me not to unmask him. He said he was a rich man and offered me money and jewels, and a number of paintings that he claimed—truthfully, as it turned out—were valuable works by Mabuse and other famous Flemish masters. He also offered me a painting by Giorgione that he had told you and Pourbus was his own work. Anything I wanted if I kept my silence. I agreed, but only on condition that he also destroyed that absurd canvas with its sketch of my foot. And so you see it was I who caused him to burn the canvas—an act that resulted in him burning down his entire studio and dying in the process.

And as for the nonexistent Catherine Lescault, Frenhofer had bragged about his fictitious mistress so effectively in the taverns he frequented that he convinced his listeners that she was real. After Frenhofer died, I instructed my cousin to spread reports of her departure from Paris as the result of an incident with a nobleman. False rumors about a beautiful woman, even when she does not exist, are easily believed and easily spread in a city like Paris. Indeed, I am sure there were several young noblemen who happily claimed to be the ones responsible for her departure. The mythical Catherine had everyone fooled, including you. You may also recall my cousin. Under my instruction, he also pretended to assist you in your search for me and drew you into the conclusion that I had been murdered and my body disposed of in the Seine.

A few days after Frenhofer's death I also confronted Master Pourbus. I told him that I knew he owed Frenhofer considerable sums of money and how he was complicit in the scheme to sacrifice me to Frenhofer's perverted desires. Public knowledge of this scandal would ruin his reputation. Indeed, some might even speculate that it was Pourbus himself who had killed Frenhofer in order to escape his debts. At first, Pourbus tried to laugh me off saying that nobody would take the word of a foolish young girl against that of

Marie de Medici's painter. I said that might be so, but there was one person who would believe me without question, and that was you, my dear Nicolas. I told Pourbus that if you learned of his complicity you would not hesitate to kill him. And if he doubted my words he only had to recall how you had stood ready to kill Frenhofer just a few days before. Pourbus recognized the danger he was in and that I had the upper hand. He asked me what I wanted for my silence. I said that the first thing I wanted was for him to tell me everything he knew about Frenhofer, and the scheme to lure me into his studio.

Frenhofer's story, as told to me by Master Pourbus, was quite remarkable. Frenhofer was the son of a successful merchant from Ghent from whom he had inherited a considerable fortune. Nothing was known about Frenhofer's mother. Frenhofer was something of a prodigy, but because of his wealth he could do what he liked and became a dilettante and intellectual gadfly. He enjoyed the company of artists and used his wealth to buy their friendship. From them he learned about painting and sculpture, and developed sophisticated theories about art and the creative process. He also possessed considerable artistic talent of his own and could show flashes of genius when he felt like it. But because he didn't need to earn a living he didn't develop his skills.

When Pourbus was employed at the court of the Duke of Mantua he had met Frenhofer by chance, in a brothel. At the time, Pourbus was losing commissions to his rival Rubens, and was running up considerable debts. This made him *easy prey for Frenhofer's apparent generosity. As Frenhofer insinuated himself into Pourbus's life he revealed his darker side: perverted sexual desires that he would go to great lengths to gratify. Indeed, his licentious pursuit of the youngest daughter of one of Mantua's most influential courtiers forced Frenhofer to flee to Paris. This occurred at about the same time that Pourbus himself had moved there. Frenhofer was also a fantasist and decided he would pass himself off in Paris as a student of Mabuse—a somewhat risky venture since he would have had to be impossibly old for this to be true. Nonetheless, he relished the role of ancient genius and costumed himself in the clothes of Mabuse's time, and contrived stories about Mabuse based on biographies of Flemish artists from that period.*

Pourbus told me more about Frenhofer's unusual artistic genius. If you gave him a pencil and paper he could, in a few deft strokes, draw a goblet you would want to drink out of, or a hand you would want to shake. Give him a small canvas and a palette full of colors he could create, with a few quick daubs, a plate of fruits so luscious you would want to eat them. But ask him to create a large-scale composition, such as a biblical scene, from scratch and he would freeze up and be incapable of even starting it. It was his lack of formal training, self-discipline and, Pourbus suspected, a certain lack of self-confidence that was the reason for this. But give him a completed picture and he could transform it into something far beyond the original painter's abilities. If Catherine Lescault had really existed, Frenhofer could not have painted her. But if he, Pourbus, had painted her for Frenhofer, Frenhofer could have transformed her into a living beauty. Pourbus showed me his "Mary of Egypt" and explained how Frenhofer, as you had witnessed, had transformed it. Even I could tell it was a masterpiece. I almost felt sorry for Pourbus when he said that Frenhofer had ruined his painting because he had made it so much better than anything he could have created, and no one would believe it was his own work. The painting was destined to stay hidden from sight and serve as a cruel reminder to him of his own artistic limitations.

Pourbus then explained the matter of that sordid visit to Frenhofer's studio. Apparently, Frenhofer had seen us together on Rue de la Harpe and immediately began to obsess about me and follow me. At the time he didn't know who you were and it was only by chance that he met you in Pourbus's studio. Realizing that you were a young artist of great talent and greedy for success, but also a naïve and impressionable youth, he immediately hatched his diabolical scheme. All that talk about Catherine Lescault and the need to see living beauty personified was a wicked ploy for you to give me up to him. After that first meeting with you, he made Pourbus continue to manipulate you, and convince you that Frenhofer would reveal his non-existent masterpiece of Catherine in exchange for me. To think, my dear Nicolas, we were all victims of that evil genius: Pourbus because of his debts, you because of your artistic ambition, and me because of my love for you.

21

My meeting with Pourbus ended with a hard, cold bargain. I told him that he had my silence in exchange for "Mary of Egypt", some of his other pictures, and the promise that he would terminate his relationship with you—for I sensed he was a man of moral weakness who would be a bad influence. I left Paris the next day a rich woman.

I begged Gillette to stop. Her tale had left me emotionally drained. I felt immense shame over my responsibility for her degradation by Frenhofer and, at the same time, I was overwhelmed with wonder at her enormous courage and strength that I had failed to recognize in my youth. I also felt a great sense of relief on finally understanding all those unanswered questions that had plagued me all those years ago: why Gillette had disappeared without a trace, why we could never find Catherine Lescault, why Pourbus had pretended to have destroyed *Mary of Egypt,* and the meaning of that perfectly drawn foot on Frenhofer's canvas. And now I also understood why Pourbus had turned his back on me after Frenhofer's death. How grateful I now was to Gillette for making him turn me away. If I had become his pupil, his old-fashioned Flemish style would have ruined me as an artist.

In tears I asked Gillette to forgive me for all my failings. She laughed and said she had forgiven me long ago. We had been so young and naïve in those days, and so much had happened in our lives since then that none of those distant events mattered any more. I then asked her to continue with her tale and explain why she had resurrected Catherine Lescault.

After I left Paris, I assumed the identity of a young widow. It is ironic that being a widow has its advantages—for one is accorded far more respect than one receives as a single or married woman. For the first year after leaving Paris I travelled around Europe, discreetly selling some of the jewels and smaller paintings I had obtained from Frenhofer. My claim that they had belonged to my late husband aroused no suspicion.

I then settled in Amsterdam. There I found a circle of young artists who I befriended and supported by buying their work for quite modest sums. Many of those artists are now acquiring considerable fame and their paintings and prints are much sought after. In return for my patronage they taught me everything they knew about art. Of course, they all wanted me to pose for them but I refused to do so. I wanted to preserve my reputation as a widow of unblemished character. Although I had little artistic ability of my own, I had a good eye and quickly became skilled at recognizing talent and works of value. This enabled me to become a successful art dealer. However, I was well aware that a female dealer, especially one of my relative youth and, dare I say it, beauty, would be the subject of too much curiosity and gossip. This being so, I employed the services of a lawyer to represent me, to become the face of my business. He was a fine man with a well-deserved reputation for integrity and business ability. He soon fell in love with me and asked me to marry him, which I did. In some ways it was a marriage of convenience, but it also proved to be a marriage of kindness and friendship. It was also a perfect business partnership. Our wealthy clients were pleased to deal with a man known for his honesty and, at the same time, they enjoyed showing off to his beautiful wife by flaunting their wealth. They readily paid the prices we asked and our transactions were always conducted on the most cordial terms. As our business grew I was able to sell, without suspicion, the larger works that I had obtained from Frenhofer and Pourbus. But "Mary of Egypt" was never for sale. Indeed, it was never seen.

My husband died suddenly two years ago. It was a great blow and I then learned the true suffering of widowhood. My great comfort has been my daughter—a wonderful and intelligent young woman with great musical talent. Her name is Nicola.

It was after my husband died that I resolved to contact you. Although I had followed your illustrious career I felt no good could come of contacting you while we were both married. And after I became a true widow, I knew that contacting you directly in Rome would invite gossip and rumor mongering in a city where those popular pastimes could damage your reputation. This is where "Mary of Egypt" and Catherine Lescault came into play. I had heard of Count S.'s interest in expanding his collection of Flemish masters and determined to sell him the picture under the guise of Catherine. For me it was a ploy to attract your attention. You were the only other living person who had seen the painting and, after the best part of thirty years, I was confident that you were the only person in Rome who would recognize the name Catherine Lescault.

The Count was too keen on purchasing "Mary of Egypt" and too busy trying to seduce me to worry about how I had acquired the painting and who I was. To him I was just a beautiful widow with a picture to sell. However, he was well versed in Flemish art and when he expressed some surprise at the exceptional quality of the painting it was an easy matter for me to mention that the illustrious Nicolas Poussin, the most famous painter in Rome, had known Pourbus in Paris and could, perhaps, be consulted for an opinion. By also telling the Count that I was going to Paris and knowing, through my connections in de Noyers circle, that you were about to be summoned to France, the trap was laid. It was a test: if you did not take the bait and enquire after Catherine Lescault in Paris, I would know that you had forgotten about me. The sale of "Mary of Egypt" also marked the end of my career as an art dealer. I had amassed a small fortune and was determined to spend the rest of my life devoted to the best interests of my daughter.

And so, my dear Nicolas, you took the bait and now we are here—together again after almost thirty years.

I again asked Gillette to pause and allow me to absorb her extraordinary tale and marvel at her genius. I had many questions to ask, and also the desire to tell her something of my own life. We took some refreshment and spent the rest of the evening like old friends sharing our memories and dreams. When I returned to my apartment that night I slept more peacefully than I had for many a year. When I awoke the next morning, I realized that she had never told me her married name and how I might contact her again. I immediately went back to her residence but found it to be shuttered. Nobody in the neighborhood knew of the identity of the veiled lady who had briefly resided there.

I never saw her again. In the years that followed, Gillette became, again, my muse—albeit a secret one. No one will know about her until they read these pages, pages that I have arranged to be hidden until long after my death. But more than being Gillette she became, in my mind, my version of Catherine Lescault: a mythical woman of incomparable beauty that no artist—not even me—would ever be able to capture on canvas. And more than her physical beauty it would be impossible, in a mere painting, to express her bravery, genius and moral courage. The only artist who might have been able to achieve that, had I given him the template to work on, was Frenhofer. I thank God that he never had the chance to do so.

Nicholas Poussin, Signed this day of our Lord, November 18, 1665, Rome.

TABLE TALK

*"**I** was very disappointed in Robin's funeral."*

As a waiter I often overhear snippets of dinner-table conversation, and some can be very intriguing to say the least. When I approach a table the diners will break off their conversations to engage in the official business of the evening—ordering their meal. When I return to the table to serve a dish, answer questions, field the occasional complaint, offer a solicitous enquiry about their satisfaction with a particular menu item, discuss dessert, exchange empty pleasantries, another thread of conversation—or perhaps the same one—will be broken again.

A good waiter should be of pleasing appearance and impeccable manners. A good waiter will overhear everything while apparently overhearing nothing. A good waiter will be omnipresent while apparently being invisible. And, of course, a good waiter will have eyes and ears in the back of his head. But an even better waiter—especially a head-waiter such as myself—is one who can project an air of effortless authority that will make his customers crave his approval. Subtle body language and facial expression are everything. A theatrically pained expression in response to an injudicious choice of dish or wine is quite unnecessary when the fractional raising of an eyebrow, the subtle tightening of a smile, the slightest tilt of the head can say it all. I enjoy practicing these fine arts of silent communication in front of a mirror, and I'm often struck by how a carefully choreographed silence can induce the release of far more information than a direct question.

My wife, Amy, is lying on our living-room sofa. The coffee table is piled high with knitting. She's been knitting a lot recently, especially bed-socks. She makes room for me on the sofa and we start playing a game we call *conversus interruptus*. It's a game of interpolation and speculation: what were the diners talking about when I approached their table? How will their conversation continue after I've left? Can Amy and I join the fragments and reconstruct the entire thread of the conversation, if not the life stories of the diners themselves?

"'I was very disappointed in Robin's funeral'. Was that it? Did you catch anything else?"

"No, that was it, Amy. They immediately dropped the subject and we started to discuss the menu. The usual story."

"Who were they?"

"There were three of them, two men and a woman. Probably in their late thirties or early forties. One of the men was clearly older than the other two. An affluent bunch.

The woman was very smartly dressed. It was the younger man who said he was very disappointed."

"Hmm…do you think they were all related in some way? Three siblings? A married couple with a brother-in-law? A gay couple with a sister or an ex-wife? A ménage-à-trois? Three old friends reunited at Robin's funeral? Three strangers who had met for the first time at the funeral? Why was the younger man so disappointed? And who was Robin? Boy? Girl? Spouse? Lover? Brother? Sister? Friend? Foe? A next-door neighbor? Did anything happen next to offer any clues?"

"No. They just wanted to hear the details of our new tasting menu."

I re-enact the scene. This is something I really enjoy doing. Amy and I don't get out very much these days and we enjoy "dining out" at our virtual restaurant at home. I like to describe the dishes to my diners with the earnest air of one expert speaking to another—this strokes the diners' egos and boosts their sense of having my approval—lightly garnished with a dash of evangelical zeal.

"Our Fall tasting menu is presented as a gastronomic play in three acts: Breakfast, Lunch, and Dinner with, respectively, one, two, and three courses; and followed by a fourth act of Just Desserts. We combine the farm-to-table approach of using the freshest local ingredients with a judicious use of molecular gastronomy techniques. Our Breakfast dish, that we call Benedictus, consists of a lightly toasted miniature

muffin made of truffled polenta topped with a medallion of Maine lobster and a poached quail's egg drizzled with a Yuzu hollandaise, and served with a small cube of slow-roasted pork belly. And for those who feel that no breakfast dish is complete without coffee, the plate is garnished with three small pearls of black coffee made with a rare Panamanian geisha bean. Our executive chef is a friend of the plantation owner and we're the only restaurant in the city to obtain a consignment of this year's crop."

"The older man said, 'Ah, coffee and bacon, a blessing indeed'. The woman said, 'A little bit of everything. I think Robin would have enjoyed this.' The younger man chimed in, 'Especially the lobster', and the older man muttered 'Indeed', but there was a definite note of sarcasm in his voice. My look of polite enquiry was too much for the woman to resist telling me that 'Robin was a dear friend of ours'."

"Our suggested wine pairing is a sparkling Grüner Veltliner from Sektelleri Sziget. It's clean and crisp with delicious flavors of citrus and river rocks that perfectly cut through the richness of the dish. Of course, our sommelier can also suggest an alternative pairing such as a Franciacorta. With its perfumed hints of chlorophyll and vanilla it goes well with this, or any of the other dishes, if that would be of interest. And before you start your meal, may I offer you a glass of champagne? I particularly recommend our Billecart-Salmon Brut Reserve. I'm sure you will appreciate its lovely notes of citrus and biscuit, and long finish."

"At that point the woman said, 'That was Robin's favorite champagne'. The older guy rolled his eyes and growled, 'And last year it was Dom Perignon'. They all took the champagne and as I walked away from the table the woman and the younger man clinked glasses and drank a toast 'To Robin'. The older man did not. When I returned with the *Benedictus* I overheard the younger man say, 'She was mad about his dress'."

"*His dress!* You must be kidding me, Richard. So who's the 'she', and who's wearing the dress? Does the 'his' refer to Robin? If so, does this mean Robin was a cross-dresser, and the casket was open for viewing and he was wearing a dress?"

"A cross-dressing corpse, Amy? I doubt it. Maybe the 'his' referred to someone else at the funeral? Maybe Robin's wife?"

"Then I suppose that would mean Robin was a man and his gay partner came to the funeral wearing a dress."

"But think of the other possibilities, Amy. Robin was a woman and her husband was a cross-dresser. Or her husband was a woman that the 'she', whoever she was, referred to as 'he'."

"Maybe out of spite?"

"Or maybe 'he' was just someone else. A friend of Robin or the partner of a friend of Robin."

"But who's the 'she', Richard? And why was she mad about the dress? Maybe she was Robin's ex-wife and didn't like the fact that Robin's current partner, the cross-dresser, came to the funeral wearing a dress. Perhaps exactly the same one that she was wearing?"

"But can we even be sure about the 'mad'? Is it 'mad' as in angry, or 'mad' as in really likes?"

"I don't know, Richard. Maybe it has nothing to do with Robin's funeral at all, and they were talking about a male fashion designer's dress at a show that at least one of them, or a mutual friend, had been to?"

"That's an interesting possibility. Then the 'mad' would probably mean that 'she', whoever she was, really liked the dress."

"On the other hand, maybe she was a rival fashion designer, and she was mad about 'his dress' because she felt that one of her own designs had been undercut at the show."

"Time out, Amy. I think we're about to get lost down a rabbit hole. What have we really got so far? To be honest, not a lot. Three diners connected to each other in some way, and all of them knew someone called Robin, an apparently 'dear friend' whose funeral disappointed one of them. Robin presumably had fairly sophisticated tastes and liked lobster. But then so do most people, as does our cat, for that matter. To me, though, the most interesting thing was that sarcastic 'Indeed' from the older man and his eye rolling over the champagne. Perhaps he had some reservations about Robin, while the other two seemed to remember him or her more affectionately."

"That's definitely plausible, Richard, but to me the real problem is the business with the dress. If it's connected to

Robin's funeral we have quite a story to unravel. If it's not, then we have two separate stories to sort out."

I pour myself a glass of wine and roll a joint for Amy. She draws on it and resumes our game. "So, tell me all about the Lunch portion of the menu. Did it reveal anything more about Robin and the diners?"

I go back to playing the waiter and act out the next scene of our gastronomic play.

"*The Lunch courses are Chef's take on soup-and-a-sandwich with a salad. The soup is juniper scented roast fennel and chestnut, garnished with fennel fronds and a drizzle of Argan oil. The sandwich is a miniature brioche bun, toasted, with a slice of seared foie gras and shaved pickled fennel. We make our own brioche, of course, with specially imported French T55 flour. I'm sure you will immediately notice the authentic brioche texture. You only have to visit Eric Kayser on Rue Monge to know the difference.*"

"Richard, you are such a snob! You couldn't resist sticking that in, could you? How did that go down?"

"They all smiled knowingly, but I've no idea if they knew what I was talking about."

"*Our suggested wine pairing is Le Haut-Lieu Vouvray demi-sec from Domaine Huët. Fruity but balanced with acidity, a perfect foil to the foie gras. This is a wonderful wine that resonates in the mouth with a subtle but persistent energy that ripples through its finish.*

"*The salad is Chef's brilliant play on a garden salad. The garden consists of a 'lawn' of assorted micro-greens with a 'flowerbed' of grated, roasted golden beets planted with edible flowers, and a 'hedge' of chevre foam with shaved pistachio foliage. The garden is lightly dressed with a shallot vinaigrette using twenty-five year old Spanish sherry-wine vinegar and hazelnut oil. The nuts and the vinegar just beg for the clean sherry pairing of Lustau Fino Jarna, dry, light and mildly acidic. The salad presentation is an absolute work of art. So much so that you may not want to eat it."*

"That line always gets a smile or a laugh. Later, when I approached the table with the soup and foie gras sandwich, I overheard the woman say 'I wonder why so few people showed up' and the younger man said 'You know why,' and the older man said 'We all know why, if we're honest.'"

"Now that's much more interesting, Richard. Whoever this Robin was, it sounds as though he or she was something of a controversial figure. Maybe Robin was a con artist who'd ripped everybody off."

"Could be, Amy. Or maybe Robin was the fashion designer who'd stolen everybody's designs."

"But then there could be a much simpler explanation. Maybe the funeral announcement had been late in getting out and only a few people found out about it in time to attend. And the two men's comments were a way of blaming the woman who had been responsible for arranging the funeral."

"On the other hand, it might have had nothing to do with the funeral at all. Maybe it was the turnout at the fashion show where the infamous dress made its appearance.

However, there is something else. When I served the salad the woman said to me, 'This really is as beautiful as you said it would be'. Then she turned to the younger man and sighed 'Robin so liked pretty things'. The younger man said 'Robin liked a lot of things', and the older man snarled, 'Too many things, if you ask me'."

"There's definitely a pattern there, Richard. The older guy doesn't like Robin. The other two do. Now tell me what happened next."

I roll another joint for Amy and start my recitation of the next part of the menu.

"Our Dinner portion of the menu begins with a dish that we call Green Eggs and Ham. Our 'egg' is an avocado mousse with a sea urchin 'yolk', served with a sprinkling of Ossetra caviar and a Mangelica ham crisp."

"At that point the older guy said 'Ah, more bacon.'"

"What is it with that guy and bacon? What's the connection between him, bacon and Robin?"

"I haven't a clue, Amy. But when I told them the pairing was the Domaine Jean Vesselle 'Oeil de Perdrix' Brut, the woman asked me to explain the name."

"An excellent question, madam. It translates to 'eye of partridge', a reference to the fact that the pink color of this pinot noir based champagne looks like that of a partridge's eyes when it dies."

"She gave a theatrical shudder and asked for an alternative pairing. I recommended the Keller Riesling von der

Fels. The younger man asked for the same while the older guy took the Vesselle…"

Amy holds up her hand to stop my recitation. She picks up one of the bed-socks she's been knitting. "Look at the heel of this bed-sock. The knitting sequence is: Row 1: k1, sl 1 pwise; Rows 2 and 4: purl; Row 3: sl 1 pwise, k1…also known as the 'eye of the partridge' stitch. So the next time you're asked about the Vesselle you can say: 'An excellent question, madam. While most sommeliers will tell you the name refers to the similarity of the champagne's color to that of an expiring partridge's eye, the true origin of the name is as follows. The vineyard owner's Latvian great-grandmother was a seamstress, and on being given a glass of the champagne she pointed out that the pattern of bubbles on the side of the glass reminded her of an old stitch used for knitting sock heels called 'eye of the partridge'. And then you can say, 'But I can assure you, madam, the connection with socks ends there. There are no sock-like tasting notes or aromas associated with this magnificent beverage.'"

"Did you just make all that up?"

"The stitch really is called 'eye of the partridge' and the rest is…well, maybe that was the pot talking. As far as I know, nobody knows the true origin of the name. Now continue with the menu, please."

"*The next course is a giant roasted morel mushroom stuffed with a crawfish and pea-sprout risotto, and served with a parmigiano reggiano cream emulsion and Meyer lemon zest. This particular risotto is made with vialone nano rice. And, of course, since mushrooms just love Pinot Noir, this dish is paired with Domaine Pierre Gelin Clos Napoléon premier cru. It has a tightly wound nose of black fruit with floral notes and a refined minerality that make it the ideal match for this dish."*

"The woman said 'I just love risotto. It was always one of Robin's favorite dishes,' and the younger man patted her hand."

"So the woman and Robin had a thing about risotto. I wonder why? Maybe they shared a plate of risotto on their first date?"

"Or maybe they performed some sort of sex acts with risotto?"

"Don't be disgusting, Richard. What a terrible waste of good risotto. Please go on."

"The final dinner course consists of sous-vide Australian lamb loin infused with pomegranate. The lamb—medium-rare, of course—is carved into medallions and served with a wasabi-spiked celeriac purée, roast Black Mission figs with a red currant-balsamic glaze, and pomegranate arils. The wine pairing is the Foradori Granato, Vigneti delle Dolomiti, an absolutely brilliant northern Italian wine with aromas and flavors of berries, pencil shavings and alpine herbs, and with a smoky end note."

"Delicious, absolutely delicious. This is absolute torture, Richard. If only I could have some of that lamb right now and a big glass of the Foradori. But, of course, I can't. So what happened during the dinner courses? Did you see or hear anything interesting?"

"It was a busy night. From what I could see, the woman and the younger man were totally wrapped up in each other. Talking to each other most of the time and making an occasional toast, while the older man seemed to be something of an outsider. However, at a couple of points during the meal he took a piece of paper out of his jacket pocket and showed it to them. They seemed very interested in what he was telling them about it.

"So, based on what I saw and heard, my take on them is this. Clearly, the woman and the younger man were very close. I'm guessing a married couple and both very close to Robin who may have had a relationship with one or both of them. Possibly without the other ever knowing. I'm also guessing that Robin was a man and it was a gay friend of his who showed up to the funeral in a dress. But I've no idea who the 'she' was who was mad about the dress. I don't think she was Robin's ex-wife. Maybe she was Robin's mother. And as for the older man, my guess is that he was a family friend and financial advisor."

"You could be right, Richard, but I'd like to hear about the dessert before I give you my take on Robin and his/her friends. Don't leave out a single delicious detail."

"Tonight's dessert offering is an exquisite miniature sacher-torte, decorated with edible gold foil, paired with a miniature passion fruit flan with a spun nougat cage. To refresh the palette, the sacher-torte comes with a tiny scoop

of a champagne-macadamia gelato, and the flan is paired with a tiny scoop of blackcurrant sorbet spiked with cassis liqueur. Our wine pairing is a late-harvest Condrieu from Les Vins de Vienne whose exotic fruity aromas, spice note, and sleek finish play up the torte and flan flavors."

"I have to tell you that the older man's eyes really lit up at the desert, but when the woman said 'Robin so loved sweet things,' his look soured."

"No doubt about it, Richard, he really didn't like Robin."

Amy draws on her joint and delivers her opinion. "My take is completely different from yours. First, I think Robin was a woman. Further, I reckon the woman at the dinner was her business partner, maybe something more. The younger man was Robin's brother and the older man was her uncle. I think the whole business about the dress was something to do with the fact that Robin was a fashion designer, and the 'so few people showed up' discussion was about the turnout at one of her shows. I simply don't believe that a man, however committed a cross-dresser he was, would show up at a funeral in a dress. That the younger man was so disappointed in the funeral probably had something to do with what the minister said. Or maybe it was about the flower arrangements. After all, Robin did like pretty things."

The following afternoon I was in the restaurant bar checking inventory. The woman from last night's dinner suddenly walked in. She said she thought she might have left her glasses case in the Ladies room. I checked the reception desk and, sure enough, there was the glasses case: an elegant red leather case with an elaborate pattern. The woman was delighted, but then looked rather wistful.

"It was a present from Robin."

"It's certainly a most elegant design and, if I might say so madam, your friend was clearly an individual of outstanding taste."

"Yes, Robin had excellent taste."

I sensed that she could be coaxed into talking some more. "I'm so sorry that you had to come back to the restaurant for the case. We would have gladly sent it to you if you had called us. May I offer you an espresso or a Pellegrino, or something a little stronger? A glass of Prosecco, perhaps? All on the house, of course."

"That's so kind of you. You know, I'd love a Prosecco."

A good waiter can also be a friend, a confidant, a counselor, and sometimes a therapist. A look of rapt attention accompanied by the occasional encouraging smile and approving nod of the head can often induce an outpouring of confidences. She introduced herself as Joanna Browning and was soon telling me about Robin as she sat at the bar sipping her drink. She told me that her fellow diners were her twin brother, Justin, and their older brother, Henry. Robin was a close friend of Justin and hers since kindergarten. They all went to the same schools and often spent their vacations together. Justin and Robin were particularly close and spent a year traveling together all over the Far East when they were students. Robin was a successful interior designer, a poet, an accomplished pianist, and stunningly beautiful. "A divine creature." The strange thing was that Joanna always referred to Robin by name so it still wasn't clear whether Robin was a man or a woman. In the end, though, life became "too much" for Robin, such a sensitive soul, and there was a "tragic end" to Robin's life.

After Joanna left, I mulled over what she'd told me and constructed a narrative of our encounter that I knew Amy would enjoy. It would make a great continuation of last night's game. But, believe it or not, about half an hour later the older brother, Henry, came in and explained that his sister thought she might have left her glasses case in the Ladies restroom. Since he was passing by he thought he would stop in and check on her behalf.

"My goodness, sir, Ms. Browning stopped by only an hour ago. We did find it and, if I might say so, what an exquisite case it is." I couldn't resist slipping in, "And I believe it was a gift from her dear friend Robin."

"She told you that?"

He seemed exasperated and I sensed an opportunity for more information. "I'm so sorry if you've been inconvenienced by coming back to the restaurant. May I offer you an espresso or a Pellegrino, or something a little stronger? A scotch, perhaps? We have a wonderful selection of small-batch bourbons. All on the house, of course."

"You know, an espresso and a scotch would be wonderful. Thank you, er…"

"Richard."

"Thank you, Richard."

He pulled a pack of cigarettes out of his jacket. This was awkward. We're a strictly non-smoking establishment, even when closed. A politely disapproving look was all that was required, and he put his cigarettes away. In addition to being a friend, confidant, counselor, and therapist, there are also occasions when a good waiter can be your best buddy. These days smokers can be made to feel like a fraternity of deranged felons. I smiled and took a gamble. "You know, sir, I could do with a cigarette myself. The staff is allowed to smoke in Chef's herb garden. If you'd care to join me, I could serve you your espresso and scotch out there."

He looked surprised, and then very pleased. My invitation was, to him, like ordering off-menu—the ultimate goal of diners who like to be recognized as special guests. Actually, I stopped smoking years ago, but I always carry cigarettes and a lighter with me for moments like these.

We went into the herb garden and sat on a small bench. I made a few remarks about the restaurant and last night's tasting menu, and asked if the scotch was to his satisfaction. He was ready to talk.

"So Joanna told you that her glasses case was a present from Robin?"

"Yes, sir."

"And did she tell you anything else about Robin?"

I sensed that the less I said, the more I would learn. "My understanding was that Robin was an exceptional individual."

"God, I wish she'd stop all this nonsense about Robin."

A solicitous look of concern on my part was all that was required to open the floodgates.

"Look, Richard, I don't know why I'm telling you this, but you need to know that Robin doesn't exist. Simply doesn't exist. Robin is a figment of Joanna's and Justin's imaginations, and usually an androgynous one at that."

I wanted to burst out laughing—if only he knew the stories Amy and I had constructed about Robin, and how wrong we'd been. I maintained my serious look and discreetly topped up his scotch. This is what I learned: Joanna and Justin were, indeed, twins, while Henry was the older half-brother. As children, Joanna and Justin lived in their own little fantasy world populated by a large cast of fictitious characters of whom Robin was the most important. They had never grown out of it. As the older half-brother, and trustee of the bequest their late father had left the twins, he had tried to wean them off their childhood game. The three of them didn't see a lot of each other but they met once a year for dinner to discuss the bequest and its investments. Whenever they met, the twins would always play their little game and spin a Robin tale—just to irritate him. They always started with a reference to Robin's fictitious funeral followed by some outlandish story about their fallen hero. Last year, Robin had been a star college football player, could have been a first round draft pick but, instead, went to a prestigious seminary. He quit after two years to join the Marines to fight ISIS. He came home with PTSD, ended up homeless, and died of a drug overdose. In another life Robin had been a natural history photographer who'd spent many years exploring the Amazon, had established a unique relationship with a previously uncontacted tribe, and had made a groundbreaking documentary about them. Tragically, though, a jealous lover had stabbed Robin to death and destroyed the film. One story or another, it always had to end dramatically.

Amy is lying on our sofa. She's smoking a joint and knitting yet another pair of bed-socks. She's delighted with what I tell her.

"This is absolutely wonderful! The things people make up. The only thing we got right was the possibility that they were siblings. I guess we'll never know what story the twins had concocted to produce that 'She was mad about his dress'. I'm sure it was outrageous. You know, after you told me about Henry coming into the restaurant, I half expected you to tell me that Justin also came in a little later, and told you that nothing Joanna and Henry had told you was true. And maybe even revealed what the dress thing was about. But that would have been too good to be true."

"Yes, I'd also wondered if he would show up on some pretext or another but, as you say, that would have been too good to be true."

"If I wasn't so tired, I'd suggest we play another round and try to guess what Justin's story would have been. Maybe tomorrow. I really need to go to bed now. Thank you for such a wonderful game."

That was one of the best *conversus interuptus* games we'd had in a long time. Amy really enjoys them. They cheer her up. She's smoking pot to help her through a really tough course of chemo. Another thing that helps—a distraction, if you will—is knitting. She and a group of friends knit bed-socks, caps, and blankets that they give to patients at her clinic. She's always been a foodie and is a real wine connoisseur. She was just starting to make quite a name for herself as a sommelier when she got sick and had to quit. And now she's completely lost her taste for alcohol and can hardly eat, or hold down, a thing. You should hear her parody of the tasting notes of the energy drinks the clinic wants her to drink: 'The subtle aromas of baby poop, the lingering, sickly chocolate aftertaste, the long chalky finish...' At the moment her diet is little more than cups of herbal tea and an occasional bowl of soup, so she particularly enjoys all my detailed descriptions of the food and wine—vicarious dining at its best. However, the good news is that her treatment appears to be working well and the outlook is promising. The doctors are talking about extended remission, if not outright recovery.

That's the good news. There's also some bad news that I don't know how to tell her. I recently lost my job—a disagreement with the owner over tipping policy—and now I'm flipping burgers at a fast-food franchise while I look for another head-waiter position. The stories I've been telling her about the restaurant recently, especially this latest one, are total fabrications. I like to think they help keep her spirits up, so I just continue with them. The funny thing is that I sometimes have the feeling she knows that I'm making them up, and maybe even knows that I've lost my job, but she keeps the game going for both our sakes. I sometimes wonder who's helping whom.

BRIGHT STARS

There's something about old bookshops. It starts with the front window with its patina of dust and the display of carelessly arranged books; some open to a page that has never been turned, some in sets that refuse to be parted. The door, a little stiff on its hinges, triggers a bell whose ring resonates beyond its allotted time. And then, as the door slowly creaks back to its resting place, one starts to breathe in the faint odor of old books, the decaying corpses of long gone minds and lost lives. Lives recalled, lives rejoiced, and lives reviled. And perhaps, lingering in the air, there's a whiff of tobacco from a just-departed customer or the perfume of a mysterious patron—transient bibliophiles as ephemeral as faintly vanishing clouds. But above all, it is the smell of the books that pervades the shop and permeates one's mind, a musty kiss that lingers on.

Every book has a story to tell. A book has a history and its owner has a past, a past that may be a story in itself that he or she may not want to be told. And a book has many voices of its own. The inner voice of its narrator and characters—the timeless voices that speak to readers across generations and continents. But old books also have their outer voices: the voices of those who type-set it, bound it, sold it, delivered it, talked about it, reviewed it, hid it, and sometimes destroyed it. They too have a role, echoing the times in which the work was written, how it was regarded then, how it is regarded now. They may be dead voices but they still linger, connected by chains of unknown events.

Open the book, feel and smell the fading paper, the worn bindings, the decaying glue—the visceral signatures of old books. If the book has not been opened for a long time—maybe years, decades or even centuries—it might retain the odors of that bygone era: a smoke-filled study, a lady's drawing room, a sea-trunk from some long forgotten voyage. Perhaps it sat on the precisely ordered shelf of a collector who prized the display more than the content, or perhaps it was the lone, prized possession of one who had fallen on hard times and sold it to ward off starvation or eviction.

My musings on the romance of old bookshops were soon interrupted. A man emerged from a room at the back of the shop to ask if I needed any assistance, if I was looking for anything in particular. A question accompanied by a sardonic twinkle of the eye, perhaps implying his suspicion that I was looking for Victorian pornography. He was one of those greying men who are always there, who have always been there—a fixture as permanent as the dusty display of books in the window. A man with an old cardigan, a wrinkled shirt, bushy eyebrows in need of a trim, a deliberately absent-minded manner hinting at an education beyond mine. The owner? A long-time assistant? An indentured slave daily released from nocturnal bondage in a cellar below? Or perhaps he is just another book, a book in human form? In an instant I've been assessed, catalogued, my mind read, and approval is pending.

"We have a nice selection of old biographies you might find interesting."

How did he know I collected biographies? That I was a collector of lives, lives whose stories have never been completely told. Lives with little gaps conveniently overlooked—gaps like the shadows cast by a partially shuttered window, the shadows that hide little truths and lies that are best forgotten.

He pointed to a set of shelves near the back of the shop. "Our biography and memoir section. Please feel free to browse. With care, of course."

The first thing that caught my eye was a small pair of brown leather-bound volumes: *Works of the Late Dr. Benjamin Franklin; Consisting of His Life Written by Himself; Together with Essays, Humorous, Moral, and Literary, chiefly in the manner of the Spectator. In two volumes, and sold by J. Hatchard, Bookseller to her Majesty, Piccadilly. 1802.* Written inside in a neat hand, in ink diffused with age, was a just legible name and date: *Dorothy M. Ferrier, June 1924.* The book's author is celebrated as a man who rewrote history while the one-time owner—one of an unknown succession of hands that held this work—is completely unknown to us now. What was the journey of this pair of books that have stayed together like a faithful couple for two centuries? How did it end up in this old bookshop in Bath? And what of Dorothy Ferrier about whom the only certainty now is that she is dead? Did she lose her fiancé at the Somme? Did she buy the set for herself? Were they a gift from a friend, a lover, or a spouse? And why this particular set of books? We can only imagine.

I then examined a single volume with badly cracked binding: *Memoirs of Moses Mendelsohn, the Jewish Philosopher; Including The Celebrated Correspondence on the Christian Religion, with J. C. Lavater, Minister of Zurich. By M. Samuels. London: Longman, Hurst, Rees, Orme, Brown, and Green, Paternoster Row. 1825.* At the top the title page was an illegible name. The only readable part was *"Rev. M…"* The possibilities were endless. Perhaps the Rev. M., a tired old cleric with a spine as creaky as the volume in my hands, had earnestly studied that long forgotten theological debate and wondered if he, the Rev. M., to the Glory of God, could have done better, could have persuaded that follower of the Abrahamic persuasion to recognize The One True Faith. On the other hand, the Rev. M. might have been an ambitious young minister seeking advancement—employing his charms and little nuggets of wisdom taken from the book to impress the marriageable daughters of the local gentry. We will never know. We never do.

For a while I'm diverted by a handsomely bound set: *Curiosities of Literature Consisting Of Researches in Literary, Biographical, And Political History; Of Critical and Philosophical Inquiries; And Of Secret History By I. D'Israeli, In Three Volumes. London: John Murray, Albemarle Street. 1823.* A dilettante's delight full of essays with titles as varied as *Of A History of Events Which Did Not Happen, On The Ridiculous Titles Assumed By The Italian Academies,* and *Secret History Of Authors Who Have Ruined Their Booksellers.* One could easily imagine the scene at a Victorian gentleman's club: self-important men, flushed and flatulent, detumescing with cigars and port after a substantial dinner of oysters, turtle soup, stewed eels and saddle of mutton. Men outbidding each other with witticisms and arcana gleaned from Isaac D'Israeli's popular work, and larding their slightly slurred conversations with gossip about the author's famous son. But now those once-popular volumes are just another curiosity of literature in their own right.

I was just about to leave when I noticed a small, slim volume with faded red leather binding and gold trim squeezed in at the end of a shelf: *A Portrait Of A Lady, A Memoir With Confidential Histories, By A Gentleman. Hepworth and Billington, London, 1820.* On the dedication page: *There comes a time in the life of a gentleman when he must record for posterity his experiences of love and by so doing offer instruction to young men seeking to understand the charms and caprices of the fair sex and save them from being dashed on the rocks of Scylla.*

"The Franklin set is now quite valuable and the D'Israeli is a rare first edition...an entertaining work."

I could have sworn that the owner or assistant, or whoever he was, had disappeared into the back of the shop after he had invited me to browse, but somehow he seemed to have followed my every move.

"But I see you've also found *A Portrait Of A Lady.* An unusual volume. It's been sitting here for a long time."

I asked him if he knew anything about the provenance of the book apart from when it was last bought and sold—usually the only information a book dealer might keep. I was pleasantly surprised to learn from Clive Burton, as he had now introduced himself, that the shop had prided itself "for generations" on keeping the best possible records of their acquisitions. Of course, he explained, in many cases the customer knew little about the books they were hoping to sell. More often than not they were simply trying to offload a pile of books cleared from the shelves of a deceased relative. But occasionally more information would be forthcoming, especially if it involved a book belonging to a favorite aunt, or an old set that looked valuable. He went to an old library card cabinet and opened a drawer. Noticing my amused smile he explained that they used the "old technology" out of respect for their old books. And, of course, drawers of index cards were safe from hackers and other miscreants. He shuffled through a handful of cards.

"Hmm…I'd forgotten just how long it's been here. Since 1923, apparently. 'Purchased from nephew of deceased owner. 19th March 1923. Five pounds.' Now, come to think of it, I do recall a story my late grandfather told me, a tale that he'd heard from his father…" At that point, Mr. Burton pointed to an old, framed photograph of two men standing outside the shop. "My great-grandfather. Taken in 1912, I think. With Samuel Rosenbach. He would sometimes come here on his book-buying trips from America…Ah yes, the story. It was about some young man bringing in a book his uncle had left him. Apparently the nephew had quite a tale to tell. His uncle, an Oxford man and war hero, had served on the Western Front with Siegfried Sassoon. He'd fallen on hard times after the war, and had recently died as the result of a tragic accident. In those days that was often a euphemism for suicide. But I couldn't say for sure if the book in question was this one. It was all such a long time ago, you know. But there was something about the story, maybe it was the Sassoon connection, which stayed with my great-grandfather and made him want to pass it on. But, whatever the reason, every book has a story to tell."

Needless to say this was an irresistible tale—quite possibly embellished with the passage of time. I purchased the book and, for good measure, the Franklin and D'Israeli sets as well.

*　　*　　*

Although in poor condition, probably due to careless storage, it was clear to me that *A Portrait* had been well made. The binding and trim were of high quality, and it had been printed on hand-cut, hand-made paper. This all suggested that the book was a privately sponsored limited edition. In addition to the mystery of the author's identity, another quickly emerged: despite detailed searches, and consultations with fellow bibliophiles, there appeared to be no known record of the publishers Hepworth and Billington. One could only surmise that it had been a short-lived publishing house, possibly specializing in the vanity press for well-heeled patrons. The book might well have been a candidate for D'Israeli's *Secret History of Authors Who Have Ruined Their Booksellers.*

Even if the outer voices of the book were yielding little, I was confident of learning more from its inner voices. The dedication, promising to teach young men about the ways of love and save them from the sirens luring them to their doom, suggested a well-educated and probably overwrought member of the privileged classes wallowing in the romantic zeitgeist of the day. The text itself might reveal, through some casually dropped detail, the identity of the lady in question if she existed at all or, at least, the social circles in which she and the author had moved.

In fact, revelations were immediate. The first chapter, *On Beauty*, opened with: "A thing of beauty…" Was this a coincidence or was the author deliberately using those famous words of Keats? Predicting the past is often an exercise in tempering one's imagination, but a few conclusions that could be drawn, albeit from those first four words, were plausible. At the time of the book's publication, the year before Keats's death, the poet was still little known to the general public and poorly regarded by the critical establishment of the day. If the quotation was deliberate, the author must have either known Keats or had moved in the same social circles. But it was more than those first four words. The chapter discussed at length, with language that had resonances of Keats's sonnets and odes, objects of beauty such Grecian urns, nightingales, skylarks, the poetry of Byron and Chatterton, spring flowers and so on. Admittedly, these were all topics that the Romantics of the day rhapsodized about, but there was a definite Keatsian flavor to the writing.

The second chapter, *On the Fair Sex*, began with the words:

> *How often have we young men of pure and innocent heart been ensnared by those carefree nymphs of the downward smile and sidelong glance? Have lost our heads—nay, been reduced to gibbering fools—to the sweet pout of ruby red lips and the toss of golden curls? Mesmerized by the Zephyr breezes of flirtation only to be dashed by the Boreal winds of disappointment? Pursuing a Penelope only to discover that she is a Cressida? Beware!*

The phrase "We young men" was a valuable clue. At that time you were considered to be an old man at forty, so it was reasonable to surmise that the author was much younger, probably in his early twenties—the perfect age for pursuing Byronic fantasies. "Nymphs of the downward smile and sidelong glance" was a direct quote from Keats's sonnet inspired by his sister-in-law. Again, clear evidence of the Keats connection.

Despite its ominous warnings, the chapter mainly focused on the manners and deportment of the fair sex. There were detailed descriptions of the dances, parlor games, conversational topics, novels, and theatricals enjoyed by young ladies of the time. The greatest detail, however, was devoted to matters of dress: cambric frocks, muslin flounces, silks, gloves, white kid boots, shawls, bonnets and ribbons, so many ribbons. Dress, it seemed, in the view of the anonymous author was the bait to trap the young romantic.

> *And so, young sirs, be on your guard when millinery and fripperies are deployed. When the fair maid says: "Sir, do you not think the blue ribbon in my hair is most becoming?" this is a trap laid by the cunning Artemis. You may think you are a worldly fox but in truth you are not, for she will reduce you to a hapless little rabbit. And rabbits make for a tasty pie!*

The author's familiarity with the details of women's clothes and fashion accessories of the day suggested that he must have known a woman, or women—his sisters, most likely, or the sisters of a close friend—from whom he could have acquired such knowledge. It was now reasonable to surmise that our author was a well-educated man in his early twenties, of a romantic disposition, with a fashion conscious sister or two and most likely acquainted with members of Keats's circle of admirers, if not Keats himself.

The third chapter, *On Love*, explored the agonies and ecstasies experienced by the young romantics in their pursuit of love. Pure love, chaste love, eternal love, and that most sought after of all loves, unobtainable love. The chapter was full of allusions to, and quotes from, the great love stories of antiquity as well as references to artworks of the high renaissance such as Titian's *Sacred and Profane Love*. The author warned his reader that love would make him selfish. That he would be forgetful of everything but seeing his love again; how exquisitely miserable he would be; how he would not be able to breathe without her; and how he would never be satisfied with a thousand kisses and always crave that thousand and first. It was all the overheated rhetoric of early nineteenth century romanticism, albeit with a faintly familiar ring to it.

Any attempt at suppressing the undercurrent of sexual yearning was abandoned in the final chapter, *On Passion*. The chapter overflowed with the honey and sweet nectar of kisses bestowed on the swelling breasts and other parts of the beloved's fragrant and fully surrendered body. But then lightning struck:

> *But if you will fully love me, though there may*
> *be some fire, 'twill not be more than we can bear*
> *when moistened and bedewed with Pleasures.*

This was a direct quote from one of Keats's letters to his great love, Fanny Brawne. And that was absolutely impossible! Those now famous letters were not published until 1870, fifty years after the purported publication date of the book.

The mystery of the book's authorship was now compounded by intrigue. If, as now seemed likely, it was produced sometime after 1870, why would the author want to assign it the false publication date of 1820? What nefarious purposes could that have served? In 1820 the only two people who knew the contents of those letters were Keats and Fanny, intimate letters that neither of them would have shown to anyone else. However, the trouble was that there was another sensational possibility: the publication date was genuine and the anonymous author was none other than Keats himself! And it made perfect sense. Those familiar sounding phrases in the discussion of the perils of love were also from Keats's letters to Fanny. Furthermore, some of Keats's friends had noted that the white clad Aphrodite in Titian's famous painting looked like Fanny, and Fanny herself was a fashion-obsessed seamstress—hence those lengthy discussion of fashion in the second chapter. She even liked wearing blue ribbons in her hair! And that heated final chapter, *On Passion*, also made sense. Their love was never consummated and the chapter, indeed the whole book, must have been written to satisfy Keats's need to express all his sexual yearnings and fantasies about Fanny.

The extraordinary conclusion that the book might have been written by Keats made discovering the book's past ownership all the more important. How could its previous owners have failed to realize its literary value, or had they deliberately kept it secret? The only information available was the story Clive Burton had told me, the story passed down from his great-grandfather. Even if it was only partially true, it still offered significant clues. The previous owner, according to the nephew, had been an Oxford man, a war hero, and had served with Sassoon. The third fact was key: it revealed that the owner had served with the Royal Welch Fusiliers. The privileged young men of Oxford and Cambridge sent to their doom in the Great War usually enlisted as junior officers, typically as Second Lieutenants; maybe rising to Lieutenant or Captain if they survived. To an adoring nephew, an uncle serving on the Western Front was a hero, but this also suggested the possibility of a military decoration such as the Military Cross, a decoration reserved for junior officers at that time.

Identifying the unknown uncle was surprisingly easy. The death of an Oxford man who had served as a junior officer in a famous regiment and had likely been awarded a military decoration would have almost certainly been recorded in the Births and Deaths column of the old London Times. That old filing card in the bookshop told us the year, 1923, and probably the month, February or March. Working through the newspaper's archives I found several candidates but only one, reported to have died on 23rd February 1923, had served with the Royal Welch, had been awarded an MC and was a MA(Oxon). His name was Richard Augustus Howard. Claiming that I was writing a family history and wanted to learn more about "my distant relative", I was able to learn from Oxford University that he had been a Fellow of Exeter College. The college bursar was happy to help and within a week had found a brief obituary of him in the college archives.

> *It is with much regret that we record the pass-ing of Richard Augustus Howard MA, one-time Fellow of Exeter College. Richard, born in 1886, was the younger son of the Honorable Stephen Howard, a second cousin of the Duke of Grafton. He attended Charterhouse where he achieved academic distinction, winning poetry prizes and becoming a member of the Apostle House. In 1904 he entered Exeter College where his father and grandfather had both been students before him. A first in English led to an MA in 1910 by which time he had become an English tutor at Exeter special-izing in the poetry of the Romantic Movement. In 1913 he was made a Fellow of the College. A*

brilliant academic career was cut short, as it was for so many, by the outbreak of the Great War. He enlisted as a Second Lieutenant in the Royal Welch Fusiliers, serving on the Western Front for most of the war. It was during that time he met the controversial war poet Siegfried Sassoon. In 1916, he was awarded the Military Cross for conspicuous gallantry during a daring raid on enemy lines and was mentioned in dispatches on several occasions. In 1917, while on leave from the front, he became engaged to the noted beauty and socialite Cynthia Hixby-Hughes with the intention to marry after the war. Sadly, the end of war only brought tragedy: his older brother, Major Giles Howard DSO, was killed a few days before the Armistice, and both his fiancée and his mother died of the Spanish Flu a few months later. He returned to Oxford in 1919 to resume his duties as a tutor and to work on a biography of Keats. In 1920, the death of his father in a riding accident and the need to sell the family estate to settle a legacy of substantial debts took its toll and resulted in Richard resigning from the college. He essentially retired from public life and lived in a cottage on the estate of Lord Oliver Noxington, a friend from his Charterhouse days. According to Lord Noxington, Richard continued to work on his Keats biography and another book, and found peace in his hobbies of book restoration and bird watching. A tragic accident took Richard's life on February 23rd, 1923. He is survived by his nephew, Sebastian Howard.

This brief biography correlated perfectly with the story I'd been told at the bookshop. But my satisfaction in resolving the identity of the book's previous owner was accompanied by the realization that Richard Howard, an expert on Keats and book restoration, was ideally qualified to have written and produced it himself. If so, why and to what end? That he had been engaged to a "noted beauty and socialite" called Cynthia, the namesake of Endymion's love in Keats's epic poem, was striking. In fact, it was now obvious to me what had happened. For this romantically inclined poet and Keats scholar, Cynthia was to him as Fanny was to John Keats. One could imagine the heated but unconsummated embraces of Richard and Cynthia before he returned to the front. And there, crouching in his dugout, shells exploding around him, he would anguish about his "dearest girl" flirting with all those other men on leave, dashing young officers with titles and money and their inbred sense of entitlement to take whatever they wanted; to take what he was too shy to take. And he would curse his romantic idealism that had frustrated his desires, desires that she might be gratifying for other men.

Richard had not acted out the life of a tragic hero of the Romantic Movement—he had lived it. But in a cruel twist of fate it was not Richard who had died in the arms of his beloved, it was his beloved who had died alone in a hospital bed and he could not even be there to tell her that she was, and always would be, his only love, his only bright star. It was perhaps no coincidence that the "tragic accident" that took Richard's life occurred on the anniversary of Keats's death. It was as though the two couples—John and Fanny, Richard and Cynthia—had lived almost parallel lives a century apart. Fanny and Cynthia were the bright stars of those two men, men who were brothers in unconsummated passion. And both were damaged men—Keats by poor health and Richard by war. Both shared the same struggle between carnal desire and romantic love, and both felt the need to express their torment in writing: Keats as the anonymous author and Richard as the anonymous version of Keats. But which one of them was it?

Every book has a story to tell and this book had two. No doubt a careful forensic analysis and textual postmortem could have resolved the matter once and for all. But I didn't want any of that. I didn't want my discovery to be ruined and ridiculed by heartless scholars, those destroyers of beautiful dreams. I wanted both my versions of romantic love to be true. I didn't want anything to ruin the magic. So I kept my discovery to myself.

OFFICE HOURS

"**I** didn't realize Tom Petersen had left the company. Yup, old Tom and I could always agree on a good contract." He gave an exaggerated look at the sign on my desk: *Jessica Rossi, Business Manager, Olafsen Construction Company.* "So I guess I'll be doing business with you from now on Jessica, or should I be calling you Ms. Rossi?" he said, emphasizing the 'Ms.' with a hint of sarcasm.

"Please call me Jess, Mr. Strickland. Mr. Petersen always spoke very highly of you."

"Well, that's good to know. Our two boys used to play on the same little league team. Do you have kids of your own, Jess?"

"No, I don't Mr. Strickland."

His little grin of moral superiority soon changed to a frown as he leafed through the draft contract I'd given him. He rubbed his nose with a thick, stubby forefinger that matched his short stocky build. He was wearing a black Pittsburgh Steelers windbreaker over a checked shirt, its open neck showing the rim of a not so white T-shirt.

Reminded me of the way my dad used to dress, but I don't think now is the time to tell him that.

"There must surely be some mistake here, young lady. You've cut the time Tom always used to allow for completion of the job. One always needs to factor in extra time for unexpected delays. But I guess you don't know about that sort of thing. I really need to talk to Mr. Olafsen about this."

"I can assure you that Mr. Olafsen and I carefully reviewed the contract this morning and it reflects the time-frame we're under for this particular project. But..," and I give him a sweet smile, "you must know that Mr. Olafsen still considers your crew to be the best."

"Hmm…well, I won't say I won't take it, but I need to think about it." Tightly rolling up the contract in his right hand and smacking it in the palm of his left, he strode out of my office with a disgruntled shake of his head.

Nearly all the people I negotiate contracts with are men. Mr. Strickland is so typical of the older guys I often have to deal with. Young lady indeed! And as for the younger guys, they often think they can just flirt their way into a better deal, and some of them even think they can flirt their way into my pants. But I'm good at my job. I stay calm when the guys behave like jerks, and when it helps I will even do a bit of flirting myself. Nothing makes me happier than seeing the Mr. Stricklands or the Brad Pitt wannabes of this world leaving my office with nothing more in their hands than the contract I originally gave them.

That evening I went with my friend Vicki to a wine-bar we often go to. It's a popular downtown hangout for the young professional crowd on their way home from work, and even if we're in our office clothes Vicki and I always try to look our best. If I know I'm going there straight from the office I wear something a little smarter, a little sexier, to work. Mrs. Olafsen, who's the company's accounts manager, always notices and says "You're looking pretty today, honey"; while Ken, our Operations Manager, and Brad, our Logistics Manager, just grin and raise their eyebrows—although I always have the feeling that Ken is hoping that I'll ask him to join me.

My cousin, Melanie, says I pay too much attention to appearances, spend too much money on clothes, and am too quick to judge people by the way they dress. And that's what's preventing men from appreciating my true self, not that I'm so sure if I know who that really is myself. To make her point, Mel doesn't shave her legs or use make-up, but it isn't clear how much good that's done her. The last guy who appreciated her for her true self turned out to have been married. A minor detail he never bothered to share with her for over a year. Given the choices out there, I'm quite happy with being well-dressed and dating guys who aren't married and like going out to nice places.

Vicki and I soon attracted the attention of a couple of guys—one said he was in commercial real estate and the other in software development. Real Estate was tall and slim. He'd come into the bar with the jacket of his cream colored suit casually slung over one shoulder, the sleeves of his well-pressed blue shirt carefully rolled up a couple of turns, and his collar and tie loosened. Software had a stockier build and was wearing jeans, a black crewneck sweater, and a sport coat. He had curly brown hair. Real Estate looked like the sort of guy you'd like to be seen with when arriving at a party, but Software seemed to be the sort of guy you'd probably prefer to leave with. Real Estate said he thought he knew me from somewhere and, for a change, that old line proved to be true: our companies had been involved in a city project the previous year and we'd both attended a Chamber of Commerce reception at the downtown Marriott. The reception had been very boring until—and this was the bit we both remembered—the Mayor's assistant had either fallen, or been pushed, into the hotel swimming pool. For the younger crowd at that event it was all very funny. City gossip was clearly Real Estate's specialty and he was quickly entertaining us with stories of who was backstabbing whom on the City Council.

We soon found out that we were all following the same series on HBO and took bets on what would happen in the next episode. The bartender had us try his new muddled gin cocktail. Maybe things were already getting a little muddled, but I was starting to enjoy myself and felt in control of the evening. Vicki suddenly excused herself saying she'd spotted somebody at the other end of bar she wanted to say hello to, and she left me alone with our two barflies.

Real Estate, true to his profession, made a point of maintaining steady eye contact with me as we continued talking, but as the evening wore on I noticed his eyes would wander from side to side to check out other women at the bar. Software, who seemed a bit shyer and whom I was starting to like, was less direct but his eyes also started to wander; in his case up and down as he checked me out. I'm used to guys checking me out, but all their vertical and horizontal eye scanning—as though I had some sort of barcode stuck on me—was starting to make me feel a bit uncomfortable. They were going to a big party on the other side of town. There'd be a lot of fun people there. Would I like to join them? Software would drive us there in his new BMW convertible. I thought I caught Real Estate winking at Software. That wink made me a bit nervous but I was still interested in going. I'd recently had a couple of bad online dating experiences, so a party where I could actually meet people face-to-face might just be what I needed.

After another round of drinks and jokes I still wasn't sure about going, so I went to the restroom to freshen up and take a long look at myself in the mirror in the hope that would help me make up my mind. Real Estate and Software didn't notice me returning and I overheard Real Estate say, "She's definitely cute, but I reckon she must be thirty. But…" and he lent over and whispered something in Software's ear. Seeing the lewd grin on Real Estate's face, I could make a good guess at what he said.

Well, fuck you guys. Maybe you should also take a look in the mirror. You're both starting to fray a bit around the edges yourselves. Don't I see the beginnings of a bald spot and a bit of a beer belly? I looked around for Vicki to see if she could help me make a graceful exit but she was engrossed with her friend, an older guy, at the other end of the bar. I pretended that I'd just received an urgent text message and had to leave. I made my excuses and went home alone.

I was really mad at Real Estate. What a butt-hole, and what really hurt was that he thought I looked thirty. I'm twenty-eight. When I got home I spent a long time looking at myself in the mirror. I'd just started my period and that always makes my face look a bit puffy and my hair goes slightly frizzy. That must have been it. On a good day I can pass for twenty-six, maybe even twenty-five. What a day. It began with an old guy calling me a young lady and ended up with a young guy calling me an old one.

The next day at work I'm in the copy room and thinking about the previous evening. I was still mad at Real Estate and wasn't sorry I'd decided to skip the party although Software, whose name was Mike Scott, had made quite a nice first impression. I had the feeling that if he hadn't been there with Real Estate the evening might have gone very differently. Maybe I'd run into him on another occasion. Distracted by these thoughts, I dropped a folder on the floor spilling a pile of papers. As I start to pick them up Ken is suddenly there helping me. He notices that one of the documents is the Strickland subcontract.

"You know Strickland called the boss yesterday complaining about the contract you gave him. Well, you know the boss. He gave Strickland quite an earful. Told him that Tom had been fired for screwing up a number of important contracts and you were too polite to tell him that because you knew they were buddies. And you were doing a great job cleaning up all the messes Tom had left behind."

Praise from Mr. Olafsen was rarely given directly and Ken was clearly very pleased to be the bearer of the boss's compliments about me. It reminded me of an incident a couple of weeks before when, at the end of a long day, I couldn't get my car to start and suddenly there was Ken on the scene able to help out. When I made the usual lame remark about him being a knight in shining armor he looked so pleased—rather like a small kid being praised by his teacher. A bit pathetic, but also kind of sweet, and that's the funny thing about Ken. At first sight he seems like that irritating co-worker every office seems to have. He laughs a lot, tells off-color jokes, and makes sarcastic little remarks about his ex-wife. And that's probably why he's so good at working with the construction crews. But around me he's different: he becomes shy and awkward and tries to be helpful. So far he's never behaved inappropriately, but I often feel his eyes burning on my butt when I walk past him. I sometimes think that Ken and I could be friends, maybe even something more. But I'm leery of office entanglements.

I had one at my previous job and am still regretting it. So for now I'm just happy with our current working relationship. Maybe I'll save him up for a rainy day, but I just wish he'd wear better-cut pants.

Ken tells me a funny story about Strickland's foreman who has a drinking problem but who Strickland won't fire. Apparently they go back a long way.

"Strickland's a bit of an old whiner but he always delivers for us. Give him a little more time, Jess, and I'm sure you'll win him over."

We go back to our respective offices exchanging genuinely friendly smiles. Our little chat has clearly made Ken's day, and mine too.

Brad couldn't be more different. At first sight he seems like the ideal co-worker: polite and efficient, and very knowledgeable about the construction business. He's earnest and serious, or pretends to be. He likes to sit next to me at my desk—a little too close for my liking—to review our contracts. Unlike Ken, who's a bit on the heavy side, Brad has an athletic build he's clearly rather proud of. Apparently he was quite a star as a high school athlete and no doubt marrying his high school sweetheart seemed like the right thing to do, at the time. But now he hints at being unhappy at home. He sometimes asks me to go for a drink after work. I did the first time he asked when I was new at the company, but I quickly guessed his game and declined all his invitations since then. Professionally he's a good colleague but otherwise he's a man to be kept at arm's length. So there you have it: Ken and Brad—one's a good guy in disguise, the other's a bad guy in disguise, and they both want to fuck me. Vicki says I should do both of them.

Brad and Ken are standing by the coffee machine and Brad is pointing to something in the newspaper he's holding. "Hey, listen to this Jess," and Brad reads out, "A white male was found dead with a self-inflicted gunshot wound to the head in a pick-up truck at the parking lot of the Lucky J convenience store at Forrester and E. Bennett. The man was identified as Russell Wayne Morgan, 64. According to the Sheriff's Department there was evidence that Mr. Morgan had been drinking heavily. There are no known next of kin."

Ken looks at me, "That's Pete Strickland's foreman I was telling you about the other day."

Just then Mr. Olafsen walks in. He's tall, thin and stern looking, and wears old-fashioned wire-framed glasses. He's not one for idle chitchat. Brad quickly tells him what we'd been talking about. Mr. Olafsen looks grim.

"I knew Russell. When he wasn't drinking he wasn't such a bad guy and could put in a good day's work when he felt like it. He and Pete Strickland were in Vietnam together at the end. Just kids out of high school. Pete never talks about it, but he once told me that Russell came back pretty messed up."

Brad, Ken and I were all born long after Vietnam. Talk about Vietnam always sounds pretty remote to me. It was all such a long time ago, but I know it isn't for the guys who had to go. Suddenly Ken speaks up.

"That's what happened to my dad. My mom told me that he never talked about what happened to him in Nam. Then one day he and a few of his buddies went to DC to see the Wall. When he came back he didn't say a word. But a few days later he drove his truck out to a place where he used to hang out with his high-school buddies and blew his brains out. I was only ten at the time. They just told me that he'd had an accident. I guess it was seeing all those names that did it."

We all stare at Ken. None of us, not even Mr. Olafsen, had heard any of this before. Ken looks very uncomfortable and says he'll be out for the rest of the day, and most of the day after, checking on our construction sites. Mr. Olafsen walks off without saying a word but just as he's going through the door he turns to Brad and me and says, "I was there too, you know."

It's just the two of us left in the office. Brad starts talking. "I never knew any of this. Poor old Ken…and Olafsen being there too…" He looks uncomfortable and suddenly blurts out, "My dad didn't have to go, he had a medical exemption. Did your dad go, Jess?"

Our family didn't talk much about Vietnam even though my dad and some of his cousins all got called up. What I learned from my mom was that when my dad was drafted he had been working as a gas station attendant so, in their wisdom, the army decided that he was an auto-mechanic and he ended up working at a service depot outside Saigon. Never saw any combat, and by the time he was discharged he had learned enough to really call himself a mechanic. And that's how he earned his living. So, in a funny sort of way, the war worked out for him when it didn't for so many others like Ken's dad or Russell. I just said, "Yes, my dad had to go, but he never talked about it either."

We're a pretty friendly sort of firm. The usual office chit-chat and gossip and the occasional bit of personal drama, but those last few minutes were something quite different. Ken, Brad, and even uptight Mr. Olafsen, suddenly opening up about stuff they never wanted to talk about, and it was all triggered off by the news that some old guy with a drinking problem had blown his brains out. I was relieved when I heard the phone in my office ring. If it hadn't I might have started telling Brad stuff about my dad. But poor old Ken, imagine your dad blowing his brains out when you're just a kid. I often had the feeling that my dad was so bottled up that he might explode, but he never did. And maybe that's what killed him—a massive heart attack when he was only fifty-eight. All those guys of my dad's generation: Ken's dad, Mr. Strickland, his buddy Russell, Mr. Olafsen, all getting blown up and shot at for nothing. Whether Mr. Strickland liked me or not I resolved to try and be nice to him. I went to find Mr. Olafsen to see if we could make the terms of his contract a little easier. The next time I see Mr. Strickland I'll be sure to tell him that my dad was also a Pittsburgh Steelers fan.

Vicki asks me to meet her at a bar, a different one from the one we went to last time. I was glad about that. I didn't feel like running into that butt-hole Real Estate again, even if he was there with Mike Scott. Vicki and I sit at the bar with a glass of wine and start catching up when a woman comes over and says hello to Vicki. She's the assistant manager at a bank that Vicki's firm does business with and she introduces herself to me as Meredith. She exudes self-confidence. She's wearing a well-cut marigold colored jacket with black trim, a black skirt, some cool jewelry and a purse I could never afford. Looks like she's come straight from work. I'm guessing she must be in her mid- thirties. Sort of woman I think I'd like to look like when I'm her age. Vicki suddenly waves to a guy sitting in a corner by himself. She excuses herself and goes over to his table. It's the same guy she was with the other evening. When I'd asked her about him after our last outing she was kind of cagey. I'm starting to wonder if he's married. It wouldn't be the first time she's been seeing a married man.

Meredith tells me that she's with a couple of girlfriends and invites me to join them. Cecelia and Steph. Cecelia is very pretty with long blond hair and looks to be in her early twenties. She's wearing a black off-the-shoulder top and bright red lipstick. Steph is tall and athletic looking. She has this really cool short haircut—something I'd like to try for myself one day—and she's wearing tight jeans and a short leather jacket over a white T-shirt. She tells us a funny story about a guy who tried to come on to her at the gym the day before. Her guy imitations are wicked and I take an immediate liking to her. Cecelia and Steph don't look like the sort of girls who'd work at a bank, but they're obviously great friends with Meredith. Maybe they all belong to the same gym. A couple of guys come over to our table and ask us if we'd like to join them for a drink. We all laugh at them.

Meredith tells me they're going to a club where a band they like is playing. Would I care to join them? I didn't recognize the name of the club or the band but it didn't matter. I was really enjoying their company and a girls' night out was just what I needed. Cecelia, who'd been sitting next to Meredith, whispers something in Meredith's ear. Meredith smiles at her. It's a sweet smile, a really sweet smile...and suddenly it all clicks. I recognize the name of the club we're going to. It's a well-known gay bar. They're all lezzies! So that's how they know each other. Why didn't I see it sooner? Still, live and let live. About five years ago my mom's sister walked out of her marriage of twenty years and moved in with a much younger woman, and they've been together ever since. Melanie claims she's completely cool with her mom being that way. But Mel's always cool with anything that shocks her family, and that was a real showstopper for our lot. My old man never got over it and said he didn't want my auntie bringing that woman over to his house, ever. As much as I like my new friends I have a feeling that if I go with them there'll be a point in the evening when I'll have to say no to Steph, and I already like her too much to want to do that. I pull the old cell phone trick and claim I've just got a text message from my mom telling me that she's not feeling well and, of course, I need to go and look in on her. Meredith tells me to stop by the club later if my mom's OK, but I know she knows that I won't. I exchange friendly little hugs with all of them and Steph's hug feels a bit more than friendly. I did the curious thing in my senior year at high school with Fran Mitchell. It wasn't for me, and as much as I'd taken a liking to Steph that wasn't likely to change.

When I got home I took a long look at myself in the mirror. Last week I was looking at myself wondering why a guy like Real Estate would think that I looked thirty. And now I'm looking at myself wondering why a woman like Steph might think that I'm a dyke. I seem to spend a lot of time looking in the mirror these days: either to help me decide what to do, or to try and work out what went wrong. But it really gets me thinking. What am I looking for in the mirror? And then I wonder about that guy Russell who came back from Vietnam all messed up and blew his brains out last week. What did he see when he looked in the mirror? And then there was my old man. What did he see?

I've never forgotten something that happened between us a few years ago, just before he had his heart attack. I was finishing my associate's degree in business management at our local community college—not exactly Harvard, but I'd be the first in our family to get any sort of college degree.

I was doing it part-time and finding juggling my job and studies a bit of a struggle. I was having Sunday lunch with my parents and said something to the effect that I wondered if it was all worth the effort. My dad suddenly smashed his fist on the table and said, "Finish your goddamned degree Jess or you'll end up a nobody like me." He really scared me. I thought he was going to explode. When he looked in the mirror did he say, "I see Frank Rossi, a nobody"? If he hadn't had his heart attack would he have ended up blowing his brains out too? It's really time I stopped looking in the mirror for help.

A few days later I get a phone call from Mike Scott. He asks if I remember meeting him a couple of weeks ago. He tells me that he'd run into my friend Vicki and that she'd given him my phone number. Would I like to meet for a drink after work? I pretend that I'm all tied up this week but next week would be good, and we arrange to meet. I suggest Thursday. A weeknight first date is always a good idea. Whether things go well or badly one can always plead an early night for work the next day.

We meet as planned and spend the first few minutes politely sniffing each other's butts like dogs at the dog park. Mike is wearing the same outfit as when I first met him and a couple of days' worth of carefully manicured stubble on his face. I like the way he looks, although an open-neck black shirt might look even better with his sports jacket than his black crewneck. He tells me he feels he owes me an apology because he's pretty sure that when we met last time I'd overheard Real Estate say something rude about me. And that was why I suddenly left instead of going to the party with them. I just grin and we both agree that Real Estate's a bit of an asshole. Mike then says, "Your friend Vicki told me a lot of nice things about you."

"Like what?"

"Well, when we met last time you just said you worked for Olafsen Construction. But Vicki told me that you were actually the business manager there and you're only twenty-six. That's a well respected firm and that's no mean achievement."

Good old Vicki, that's why she's my best friend. I just say I got lucky. They had to fire the previous business manager and Mr. Olafsen was kind enough to give me a chance. What I didn't say was that I really wanted that job, and I'm absolutely determined never to end up like my old man and find myself looking in the mirror one day saying, "I see Jessica Rossi, a nobody." But that's not the sort of stuff I want to talk about on a first date, or even a second one, or maybe ever. However, I do need to say something more.

"Vicki's my best friend, but you shouldn't believe everything she tells you about me. For a start, I'm not twenty-six, I'm twenty-seven."

Mike laughs and tells me he's just turned twenty-nine. Almost over the hill and all that. I'm glad we got the age thing out of the way, but I wasn't sure if I was the only one who wasn't being quite straight about how old they were.

And I'm just fine with that. I feel the evening is off to a good start. We're just about to order something from the bar menu when a woman comes up to us.

"OMG, I don't believe it. It's Jess, Jessica Rossi, isn't it?"

I can't quite place her, but then I have a horrible feeling I know who she is.

"Of course you remember me, Jess. It's Fran, Fran Mitchell," and turning to Mike, "Jess and I were great friends, really great friends, at high school." This is really awkward, and before I know it Mike has invited her to join us and ordered her a glass of wine. Suddenly we're a threesome and Fran is dominating the conversation telling us her life's story. She makes up stuff about how all the boys at our high school were crazy about me, and then she drops a bombshell—well, a bombshell to me—and tells us that she married the older brother of one of our classmates, Trent Miller. But it didn't work out and they divorced after three years. Mike excuses himself to go to the restroom and it's just Fran and me.

"You and Trent's brother, Fran. I would never have thought it."

Fran laughs and looks me straight in the eye. "I know what you're thinking, Jess, but I'm straight now." And then she laughs again and pats my hand, "well, most of the time."

She then asks if Mike and I are an item, tells me that he's cute, and that I should definitely make him an item. Mike rejoins us, and our little party resumes. But now it seems that I'm the odd one out. I can't believe it—Fran is hitting on Mike and he's buying it. I can see his eyes looking her up and down, doing that barcode scanning thing. I've had enough and tell them I have to meet Mr. Olafsen at a construction site early tomorrow morning—at least that was true—and need to have an early night. Fran gives me a big hug and Mike walks me out of the bar. He says how much he enjoyed the evening and how he'd like to take me out to dinner next week. He then says he forgot to leave a tip for the bartender and asks me to wait a moment while he runs back inside to take care of it. I'm sure he will and, no doubt, exchange phone numbers with Fran.

There I am, standing on the street by myself, and I'm as pissed as hell. But I don't know whom I'm more pissed at: Mike, Fran, or myself for having misjudged a guy so badly. I'm not going to wait for him and walk off to find my car. As I'm walking along the street I pass a coffee shop and through the window I see Steph. She's sitting by herself and working on a laptop. Screw Mike. Screw Fran. Screw Steph? I go inside to say hello.

EXODUS

"Do you know what a concentration camp is? My mother won't tell me. She says they're terrible places where they kill Jews, but she doesn't want to talk about them."

That was the first question Betty Hirsch asked me after we had gone to bed and turned the lights out. There are some days, dates, events, conversations and people one never forgets. I had arrived in Vancouver on December 27th, 1938, after a train journey from Halifax that had taken almost two weeks. While we waited for our boat to depart for Australia my parents stayed at a hotel while I stayed with a family called Hirsch whose daughter, Betty, was about my age. I slept on a spare bed in Betty's bedroom. Actually, we didn't sleep that night—we stayed up the whole night talking. I couldn't stop talking. It was such a relief to have someone my own age to talk to. My words must have poured out in an incoherent jumble, especially since I didn't speak very good English; but I had a willing listener and was eager to talk.

At the time, I can't say that I knew much more than Betty about concentration camps. My parents were reluctant to talk to me about them even though my grandfather had been interned in one briefly. Soon after Hitler came to power the Nazis imprisoned opponents, real or imagined, and arrested Jews such as my grandfather who was a successful businessman. I was only ten when that happened and my mother told me that he had been forced to wear striped pajamas and peel potatoes for a few weeks before they let him out. The idea was to break him both physically and mentally and that certainly proved to be the case. Afterwards, if he was out for a walk and saw somebody in a Nazi uniform, or saw a parade in the street from his window, he would start shouting and swearing. Family members had to keep a close eye on him to avoid further trouble.

My parents and I lived in Berlin. From 1933 onward I witnessed firsthand the ever-increasing horrors of the Nazi regime, albeit through the eyes of a young girl. I may not have understood everything that was happening at the time but everything I saw left me anxious and afraid. My first direct experience of the new order occurred soon after Hitler became Chancellor. It was just before my tenth birthday. My mother had taken me shopping and on our way home we saw a crowd throwing bricks through the windows of the chocolate shop we often went to. They were shouting "*Juden raus, Juden raus.*" When we got home my mother tried to reassure me that what I had seen was an isolated incident and wouldn't happen again. A few weeks later some of my parents' friends came for dinner. They said that Hitler was a clown, that he wouldn't last, and President Hindenburg would soon dismiss him. Everything would return to normal. I remember my father saying that he wasn't so sure, and as usual he was right. Instead of things going back to normal they just got worse and worse. Within a few months my father lost his position at the hospital and most of his non-Jewish patients stopped coming to see him. By the time we left Berlin his doctor's license had been revoked and he was no longer allowed to practice medicine.

I went to a Jewish school in Berlin but after 1933 children were not allowed to matriculate from Jewish schools. Because of this, my parents sent me to a state school in 1935 so that I would have the chance of going to University. It is difficult to believe now that in 1935 we were still deluding ourselves that there was a normal future ahead of us. I was the only Jewish student in my class that year and although I wasn't subject to any blatant abuse, I felt very isolated and unhappy. After a year I went back to my original school. We had wonderful teachers there. Most of them were university professors who had been dismissed from their academic institutions. Some of the students I knew got visas to Palestine and we would go to the railway station to wave them goodbye. For us younger ones this seemed like a great adventure, and the departing children would sing and wave to us as the train left the station. Their parents couldn't stop crying as they watched them leave. I remember the occasion when the Strauss twins left: their mother ran after the train in hysterics and then collapsed at the end of the platform. I also wanted to go to Palestine but my mother said that our family must stay together.

In the summer of 1937, my father thought it would be a good idea for my mother and me to get out of Berlin for a few days, and he sent us on a short vacation to the Baltic coast. We stayed at a Jewish hotel near the sea. It was very nice, but then one afternoon a large crowd gathered outside the hotel with wheelbarrows full of stones. I remember the hotel manager reassuring the guests that nothing would happen. When it got dark, the crowd lit torches, shouted horrible things about the Jews, and threw stones at the hotel. My mother got me out of bed and told me to get dressed as quickly as possible. I still remember how frightened I was and how my hands shook as I struggled to put on my socks and sandals. We slipped out of the hotel's back entrance and hid in the woods behind the hotel until the next morning.

My father worked tirelessly to get us out of Germany and by 1938 he had obtained Australian visas for us. I would often hear my parents talking in low voices in their bedroom and sometimes I heard my mother crying. On one occasion I overheard my father tell her that there was a problem with my visa, but when I asked him if we would all be traveling together he laughed and said everything would be fine. But I had the feeling he was pretending. Every now and then at school some of the students would stop showing up, but we didn't always know why. Maybe their parents had been arrested or perhaps they had managed to get out of Germany.

As part of our preparation for immigrating to Australia, my father arranged for us to receive private English lessons. Our teacher was a Quaker, Dr. Schmidt. At the time I didn't understand who the Quakers were, and it was only years later that I learned about their efforts to help Jews escape from Germany. Dr. Schmidt gave us the lessons for free. After our last lesson we said our goodbyes. Just as he was leaving, my father pushed his best winter overcoat into Dr. Schmidt's arms and closed the front door behind him before he could say anything. I thought my father had been very rude. He explained that he could see our teacher was badly in need of a decent winter coat but that he would have been embarrassed if my father had given him the coat as a gift—so he didn't give him the chance to refuse it.

A few days later, I think it was the last day of September, my father made me listen to the radio with him. He explained to me what the broadcast was about. He said that the British had given Czechoslovakia to Hitler. I didn't understand how one country could give another country away. My father said it was a terrible thing but it had probably stopped a war starting, and because of that we would still be able to leave Germany. He said Czechoslovakia's catastrophe was our good luck.

One day in November, it was November 9th—a day I will never forget—I was coming home from school when I saw a huge mob charging down the street shouting "*Juden raus, Juden raus.*" They were smashing up Jewish shops. It was much worse than what I had seen five years before when they smashed up the chocolate shop. I saw them go into a shop, drag the shopkeeper and his wife into the street and beat them with big clubs. I think they killed them. I was terrified that the mob would catch me. I hid in a side street, and ran home when the mob had passed.

The following Friday evening we were sitting down for dinner and my mother was just about to light the Friday night candles when there was a knock at the door. There were two Gestapo men who said they had to take my father away for questioning. My father asked their permission to go to his bedroom to get a coat. When he left he kissed me on the head and said, "Don't worry, I'll be back soon." I didn't believe him. My mother said, "Let's wait until he comes back before we light the candles" and then she burst into tears. Seeing my father taken away that night was the most traumatic experience of my life.

We sat at the dinner table in a state of shock not knowing what to do or what to say. It was as though time stood still. I don't know how long we sat there, it must have been many hours, and then suddenly my father walked in. The first thing he said to my mother was, "*Liebchen*, please light the candles and let's sit down for dinner."

He told us that when he had gone into the bedroom to get his coat he had taken all our travel papers and passports with him. He knew he was taking a big risk because the

Gestapo could have taken them away and not given them back, but he felt that he could use them to save us. When he got to the Gestapo headquarters he insisted, very politely, on seeing the senior officer on duty. For some reason the two men who had escorted him agreed to arrange this. He wasn't sure why—maybe because he'd told them jokes in the car, or maybe because he'd told them that he'd been a soldier in the war. My father told us that as soon as he stepped into the Gestapo officer's room he recognized him: ten years before he had been called in as a consultant to treat the man's daughter. My father said the officer pretended not to recognize him and immediately started shouting at him and telling him that the Jews had destroyed Germany. But the more he shouted the more my father realized that he was putting on a show and was going to let him go. My father showed him all our travel papers and passports and said, "Here are all our documents. They are all in order. If you let us go we will leave Germany tomorrow." It worked. The officer said, "You have twenty four hours to leave, now get out of my office before I change my mind."

We stayed up all night packing and my father was on the phone the whole time arranging this, checking that. The next morning we took a taxi to the airport to catch a plane to Amsterdam.

At the airport all the passengers had to walk through an office next to the runway. Uniformed officials checked our documents over and over again, asked lots of questions, searched our luggage, and made us empty our pockets before they would let us board the plane. We were just about to take off when, suddenly, two men came on board and took me back to that office. They said they needed to ask me more questions, and they wouldn't let my father accompany me. And there I was back in that office all by myself with an official in a Nazi uniform towering over me. I can still remember every detail of what happened and every word he said. He gave me a nasty little smile and asked, "What's your name, girl?"

"Miriam Goldfarb, sir."

"When will you Jews ever learn? When I ask for your name you must give me your full name. The name that all Jewish girls must have on their passport."

"I'm sorry, sir. My name is Miriam *Sarah* Goldfarb."

"That's better. And what's your father's name?"

"Dr. Jacob Gold...I mean Dr. Jacob *Israel* Goldfarb."

"Hmm...a Jew doctor. Does he have any patients?"

"No, sir."

"And where are you going to, Miriam Sarah Goldfarb?"

"We are flying to Amsterdam, sir."

"I know that, you little idiot. Where are you going to after that?"

"We are going to Australia, sir. My father showed you our visas and passports before we went on the plane."

"Where's your money?"

"Money, sir?"

"All refugees have to give the Australian government lots of money when they arrive."

"My father arranged for the money to be paid by a friend of his who is already in Australia."

"Hmm…are you sure you don't have any money on you? Maybe your parents told you what to say and hid it under that pretty little blouse you're wearing? Maybe we'll have to take off your blouse to make sure you're not lying to me."

"No, sir. I swear I don't have any money. Please don't make me take my blouse off. Please let me go back to the plane."

"Come over here, Miriam Sarah Goldfarb. Look out of the window. You can see your plane on the runway. The propellers are spinning. It must be ready to take off without you. Maybe you'll have to stay in Germany. How would you like that? One minute…*Mein Gott*, there's a man running down the gangway off the plane…and he's running towards my office."

The man running to the office was my father. He'd come to rescue me. He pushed past a guard at the door and burst into the office. The officer was furious. I thought he was going to explode and he started shouting at my father.

"How dare you get off the plane? How dare you barge into my office without permission? This is all absolutely forbidden. I will have you arrested immediately. I will order the plane to take off, and you and your daughter will be left behind."

"Please, sir, let me take my daughter back to the plane. All our papers are in order. The captain says he cannot take off until all the passengers on his manifest are on the plane."

"The plane will leave when I say so. I will call the control tower right now and order the plane to leave immediately."

The officer started shouting on the phone. I didn't understand what was happening but I could see that my father did. After a few minutes the officer slammed the phone down. He was very angry and started shouting at my father again.

"You bloody Jews are nothing but trouble. Run back to the plane right now and never let me see you again. And don't forget, I can have the plane called back any time I want."

My father took my hand and we ran to the plane, up the gangway, and collapsed into our seats. My mother didn't stop trembling until the plane took off.

When we were in the air, I asked my father what had happened. "Papa, why did they take me off the plane and ask me about money and if you had any patients? I was so scared. What was he shouting about on the phone and why did he let us go?"

"They wanted to trick you. If you had said we were hiding money or that I still had patients they would have used that as an excuse to take us off the plane. They let us go because we're on a Dutch plane with a Dutch pilot. They couldn't order him around. He refused to take off without us and the control tower needed him to clear the runway to

92

let another plane land. That was what all the shouting was about. The pilot just saved our lives. We were terribly lucky."

We stayed in Amsterdam for about a week with a distant relative. After everything that had happened in Berlin it was like being on a vacation. Then we took a boat to England and a train to London. To be allowed to stay in England, we had to have a letter of invitation from an English family saying that we could stay with them. We took a taxi to that family's address. It was late when we got there and when Papa knocked on the door there was no answer. Then an upstairs window opened and a man called out to my father. Papa explained that we had their letter and apologized for arriving so late. The man at the window said, "We only wrote the letter as a formality. We didn't mean you could actually stay here. That's quite impossible. I'm sorry. Please go away." And then he slammed the window shut. When Papa got back in the taxi I heard him say to my mother in a very sarcastic voice, "It seems as though there's no room at the inn for us either."

My father always knew what to do. He had the phone number and address of a doctor he knew who had got out of Germany the previous year and had permission to stay in England. The taxi driver took us to a phone box and my father called his friend and arranged for me to stay with his family while my parents went to a hotel. After that phone call the taxi driver turned off his meter for the rest of our journey.

A few days later we took a train to Liverpool and caught our boat to Halifax. It was a miserable voyage. The sea was very rough for the whole seven days it took to reach Canada. My mother and I stayed in our cabin almost the whole time, rolling around in our bunks and throwing up. But my father was fine. He walked out on the deck and made friends with other passengers and the crew. Everybody liked my father. I sometimes think that even the Nazis liked him—perhaps it was because he was tall and had fair hair and blue eyes. Once we got to Halifax and onto our train to Vancouver we felt so much better and safer.

When our train stopped in Montreal the Jewish community there was very welcoming. They took us, and the other refugees, to a hotel to spend the night, and we were invited to have Friday night dinner at someone's home. When we left Montreal, people from the community came to the station and gave us little Hanukkah presents and candles so we could celebrate Hanukkah on the train. On each night of Hanukkah we lit the candles and sung the Hanukkah songs. I could see the candles reflected in our compartment window and, through the window, the stars and huge dark mountains outside. On one occasion, I stepped out of our compartment into the carriage corridor where I could hear other families in their compartments singing those same songs. To this day I can still hear that singing accompanied by the rattling sounds of the train as it raced through the night. I asked my father, "Papa, is this like the Exodus?" and he burst into tears. That was the only time I ever saw him cry.

At one point on the journey we stopped at a station—I can't remember its name—for a few hours and we were allowed out to stretch our legs. There was snow on the platform. Volunteers had come to the station and set up a big table piled with food that they gave us. There was a very thin and sad looking man in our carriage, and when he saw all the food he went crazy. He threw all his clothes out of his suitcase and stuffed it full of food. I think everybody was very embarrassed but nobody wanted to stop him. He must have been in a camp. Among the people handing out food was a priest with a big cross hanging around his neck. He gave me an orange, patted me on the cheek, and wished me a happy Hanukkah. I'd never met a priest before. The idea that a priest would wish a Jewish girl happy Hanukkah confirmed my opinion that the world had gone crazy.

The train journey to Vancouver was, by far, the longest journey I'd ever been on. Every time our train stopped at a station I would worry that soldiers would take us off the train. But my mother said that wouldn't happen. She said that they didn't do things like that in Canada. As each day went by I felt that I was getting further and further away from Germany, and each day I felt a little bit safer. Everybody at the stations we stopped at was very kind. Maybe it was because we were just passing through to go somewhere else. That feeling was harshly confirmed when we eventually arrived in Australia. There, we were refugees who were there to stay. "Refos," they called us. We were viewed as a nuisance and a potential source of trouble. But it wasn't just the Australians who regarded us with suspicion. Many members of the established Jewish community there saw us newcomers as jeopardizing their efforts to blend into Australian society. But, in truth, the only difference between them and us was that they had arrived on an earlier boat.

Betty Hirsch asked me what I wanted to do on my last day in Vancouver. I told her that I would just like to do something normal. Something that normal people are able to do on a normal day. I hadn't really known a normal day for the previous five years. There was always something happening that made me anxious. I told her that I wanted to go to a shop and buy some chocolate. She asked me if I thought I would go back to Germany one day. I told her that I would never, ever, go back.

* * *

All those things happened a very long time ago. Since then I've had a good life: a long and happy marriage to an Australian doctor, children, grandchildren, and a beautiful home. But scarcely a day goes by when I don't think about some aspect of our escape, our Exodus, from Germany. There were things that happened then that I didn't understand until much later. I learned that the Australian Government had cancelled my visa for some silly bureaucratic reason and it was only because an uncle of mine, who had left Germany as soon as Hitler came to power, interceded on my behalf and pledged a large sum of money to the Australian government to prove that I wouldn't be a financial burden on them. I also learned the history of that infamous Munich Agreement between Hitler and the British Prime Minister, Mr. Chamberlain. It was a truly shameful thing, but it probably saved us. History has judged Mr. Chamberlain very harshly, but I have a soft spot for him.

After the war we learned about the fate of our family. A few survived but most died in the gas chambers. One aunt stayed with her elderly parents in their Berlin apartment until they died of malnutrition, and then she committed suicide. Many years later I learned, quite by chance, that Dr. Schmidt, our English tutor in Berlin, had survived the war.

All the things that happened to my parents and me involved many remarkable coincidences and an enormous amount of luck. If any one of them hadn't worked out exactly as they had happened it's almost certain we wouldn't have survived. What if my uncle hadn't been able to sponsor me for an Australian visa? What if the mob on *Kristallnacht* had found me? What if Mr. Chamberlain hadn't made a deal with Hitler? What if my father hadn't treated that Gestapo officer's daughter? What if we'd been flying to Amsterdam on a German plane? I'll never know who that

Dutch pilot was and what happened to him. Sometimes I wonder about that kind London taxi-driver—maybe his home was destroyed in the Blitz. It all seems quite fantastic now, but everybody who survived had a fantastic story to tell. If you didn't have a fantastic story you wouldn't be here to tell it. In many ways we were luckier than most. I also think about those parents saying goodbye to their children at the railway station. They must have known that they would never see them again. Probably none of them did.

When I light Friday night candles, I sometimes think about that last night in Berlin and wonder if there will be a knock at the door. When we light Hanukkah candles I always think about that train journey across Canada. Despite the terrible circumstances it still seems like a magical time to me. Every time I get on a plane I wonder if an official will come to take me off. When I'm out in the street and see a man in uniform or hear a police siren I feel anxious. Are they coming for me? Sometimes I think that I'm always looking over my shoulder.

I can still remember how emphatic I was when I told Betty Hirsch that I would never go back to Germany. Much to my surprise, I did. A few years ago my husband was invited to a conference that was held at a resort hotel in the Harz Mountains. I had happy memories of holidays there when I was a little girl and thought I would like to go back for a visit, especially since Germany had changed so much since the war. People say it is a completely different country now. Perhaps it is. The staff at the hotel were very polite and very young—I think even their parents must have been born after the war—and I couldn't feel any anger towards them. Sometimes I would go for a walk to a café near our hotel, sit on their outdoor terrace and enjoy the beautiful views. One day I was sitting there with a cup of coffee and feeling very relaxed when an elderly couple came in and sat at the table next to mine. The man, who was tall and imposing, spoke to me in German. I pretended that I knew only a few words of German and he spoke to me in English. He was very courteous. He made small talk about the weather, asked me if I was a tourist, and welcomed me to Germany, "a most beautiful country." But all I could see was that official at the airport interrogating me, and all I could hear was *"Juden raus, Juden raus."* I got up and left. The man stood up and gave me a little bow. I'm sure he thought he was being the perfect gentleman. Maybe he was and maybe I had completely misjudged him. But some memories never leave you—once a refugee, always a refugee. I think all refugees must have moments when they feel like that.

RUSSELL SQUARE

The old-timers in Russell Square in Bloomsbury were enjoying a beautiful May morning of mild sunny weather, spring flowers, and the murmuring of the fountain they were sitting around. They were sharing the garden with a number of visitors. Some were old friends and family members, while others were just passing by. It was on a day such as this when the fleeting image of a small boy kicking a pile of leaves, a dog chasing a pigeon, a couple walking by with a pram, triggers a memory—perhaps a year old, perhaps a life-time ago, or maybe one that never existed. And so they began their daily ritual of recalling the past. But memories, like driftwood scattered on a distant beach, are picked up by waves of nostalgia, tossed and turned by the tides of time and often land on a different beach, a different reality, a different narrative.

Robin nearly always started the reminiscences. "I've never tired of London. No thinking person could ever tire of London…" and before he could get going on his childhood memories of London during the war, his old friend, Josep, would say, "Especially Bloomsbury. I've lived here for forty years, you know."

"Yes, we all know you've lived here for forty years, Josep. You always tell us that," said Nellie, who was the oldest. "I've lived here longer than any of you. I so loved living in London and Bloomsbury. So did my husband, Tom. Dear Tom, I miss him every day. There were so many interesting things to see and do, and people to meet. Why, I remember when I was a young girl meeting Virginia Woolf and Lytton Strachey here in Russell Square…"

Hannelore (Anne to her friends and family) who was sitting, as always, next to Nellie coughed theatrically.

"…Well, I didn't actually meet them, I saw them walking by together and Mr. Strachey stopped and patted me on the head. Yes, I remember it as though it was yesterday. Mr. Strachey patted me on the head and gave me a sweetie. It was a toffee."

"And you're sure it was Virginia Woolf and Lytton Strachey you saw, Nellie?"

"Of course I'm sure, Anne. You could always tell it was Mrs. Woolf by her nose and Mr. Strachey by his beard."

"Which you could have seen in countless photographs of them and their friends."

"Why are you always giving me a hard time, Anne? It was definitely Virginia Woolf and Lytton Strachey. I know it was a very long time ago, but I really did see them."

"No, I'm not giving you a hard time, Nellie. It's just important to be accurate with one's facts, even if they change with time."

"What is it with you Germans..."

"Now, now, ladies, no need to quarrel," chimed in the Reverend Pruce who was sitting nearby. "No need to quarrel on such a lovely day as this."

"Yes, Reverend. But the thing is, Anne and I like to quarrel. It helps the time go by."

Nellie turned to her other neighbor, Guido, hoping that he would enjoy her story; a story she had told him many times before. Nellie liked Guido. He was, by far, the youngest member of their group and she felt quite maternal towards him. She liked his strong Italian accent that always carried with it a hint of romance, a kiss of the hand.

"Yes, Signora, I believe you. I'm sure you met Signora Woolf and Signore Strachey in the Square, and Signore Strachey gave you a toffee."

Nellie gave Anne a triumphant smile. "See, Guido knows I'm telling the truth."

"Well, I remember London during the Blitz. One morning, after a really bad night, my parents and I went out for a walk and who should we see walking towards us but none other than Mr. Churchill himself. He was out inspecting the damage. He stopped and asked my parents if we'd been hit, and then he patted me on the head and gave me a sixpence."

"Mr. Churchill patted you on the head and gave you a sixpence, did he, Robin? Are you sure it wasn't Santa Claus," asked Paul with a laugh.

"Look, Paul, if Lytton Strachey gave Nellie a toffee, there's no reason why Mr. Churchill couldn't have given Robin a sixpence. Or rather, if Mr. Churchill gave Robin a sixpence, then Lytton Strachey could just as well have given Nellie a toffee."

"I'm not saying that he didn't, Krishna, it just sounds like a tall story to me. That's all."

"But we all like tall stories, don't we Paul? What do you think, Wendy? You're the same age as Robin, maybe you also saw Mr. Churchill during the Blitz?

"Yes, Krishna, I did. I did see Mr. Churchill. And I saw the Queen."

"And which queen was that, Wendy?" Sue, who used to love walking with her husband and two dogs in the Square, knew that Wendy often got confused and would try to help her out.

"Well, you know Sue, the one who lives in Buckingham Palace."

"You mean the one who lives there now?"

"That's right, Sue. The one who lives there now. The one who gave me my medal."

"Your medal, Wendy?"

"Yes, Krishna. I got a medal from the Queen. I'm sure I've told you about my medal before. It was the best day of my life."

"Do tell us all about it again, Wendy," said Joyce encouragingly. Joyce was a lovely lady; the friendliest member of the group, always greeting people—friends and strangers alike—and inviting them to sit next to her for a little chat.

"Yes, it was a lovely day. The sun was shining. It always shines on the best day of one's life. There were lots of people, and there was tea and cucumber sandwiches. It was the best day of my life. Did I tell you I got a medal from the Queen?"

"She doesn't always remember where she is, bless her," whispered Joyce to Krishna, "but she definitely remembers that she got a medal from the Queen. She's the only one of our group who did."

"What about me? I got a medal too"

They all stared at Fred in surprise. No one knew if that was his real name, or if he had a name at all, but they all called him Fred because it was convenient to have a name to call him by. Fred always kept to himself and rarely spoke. He was part of a group of other Freds, mysterious old-timers who were always there. Nobody knew much about them or their names.

"Do tell us about your medal, dear," said Bridget. Bridget, affectionately known as 'Super Nan', was always helpful and had been around for almost as long as Nellie.

"I was a war hero. I was at Dunkirk, and I was one of the first on the beaches of Normandy. I took out four enemy machine-gun posts. I got the Military Cross. Pinned on my chest by Monty himself."

"That's news to me," said Bridget to Jenifa, who had been a clinical psychologist, "Do you think he's making it up?" But before Jenifa could give her opinion, there was another outburst, this time from one of the other Freds.

"Military Cross, that's nothing. I got the Victoria Cross for taking out six machine gun posts at Passchendaele. I was there with Harry Patch, you know. King George himself pinned it on my chest at Buckingham Palace. See, Wendy, you're not the only one who's been to Buckingham Palace."

This was all too much for Paul. "I don't believe a word of it, either of you. There's nobody left who served in the First War, and only a few left from the Second. If either of you had won the Military Cross or the Victoria Cross you'd be really famous by now. People would be coming in all the time for your autograph. Journalists would be interviewing you and politicians would be posing for photographs with you. I think you're both making it all up. Jenifa, you're the psychologist, isn't that what old people like us do all the time?"

Fred exploded at this remark. "How do you mean, we're making it up? Of course we're making it up. All of us. Who the hell do we think we are? We're all just a bunch of park benches. And you, Paul, and Jenifa, Wendy, the Reverend, Bridget, Krishna, Sue, and Nellie are lucky enough to have a name, a plaque that says who you were, a plaque that says how people remember you and how much you enjoyed living in London. As for me, with my Military Cross, and the Fred sitting next to me with his Victoria Cross, and all the other Freds, the no-names, the nobodies that nobody knows or cares about or wants to remember, we still need to be somebody, we still need to be remembered. Maybe if we tell a good enough story people will want to remember us too. Maybe our stories are no better or worse, truer or falser, than your stories.

"When people sit on you they probably won't even notice your plaque. But a few will and maybe, just for a moment, they'll wonder about who you were and the lives you led. 'Robin...1935–2011, Never tired of London'. 'Josep...1939–2010, Resident of Bloomsbury for 40 years'. 'In memory of Nellie 1912–2004'. 'Joyce, A lovely Lady... 1931–2017'. 'To the very dear memory of Hannelore... Danzig 1932–London 2009'. 'In loving memory of Guido... Milano 1980–Milano 2013'. 'In loving memory of Paul... 1960–2004'. 'In loving memory of Wendy, MBE...1935–2010'. 'In memory of Bridget...1918–2012, our Super Nan'. 'Sue...1962–2015, loved walking here with her dogs'. 'In loving memory of Jenifa...1967–2016'. 'In loving memory of Krishna...1935–2013'. 'In memory of Reverend Pruce, 1928–2015'. All that love, all that loving memory. Why can't we have some of it as well? When somebody sits on us, the ones without a name, without a plaque, they don't think about us at all. But they should. We all want to be remembered, we all want to be loved."

But before any of the other benches could answer, there was a sudden burst of spring rain and the visitors, unwitting eavesdroppers on all those silent conversations and arguments, scurried out of the Square. If they could have heard him, they would have heard the Reverend Pruce say, as he was so fond of saying, "Well, you may think this is the end: Well, it is."

PRUFROCK REDUX

I was sitting at a seafront bar watching the sunset and observing the rituals of the dying day—parents corralling their children, couples walking hand-in-hand as they splashed through the low tide, swimmers returning to shore from their last dip of the day. And then, in the distance, I saw a solitary figure, rather thin and slightly stooped. What caught my eye was that while everyone else was in shorts or swimsuits, he was walking along the beach with the bottoms of his white flannel trousers rolled. Could it be? As he came closer, I saw that he was eating a peach. My God, it was none other than my old Harvard classmate Prufrock! I waved to him. Although it had been several decades since we'd last seen each other he couldn't avoid recognizing me and, feigning reluctance, he came over to the bar. After an awkward handshake and avoiding eye-contact, he pretended he couldn't quite recall my name, "Ah yes, er… it's been a long time, hasn't it?" I asked him to join me for a drink and ordered a bottle of wine for us to share.

I can't claim that we were particularly close during our student days. To most of us he was a remote and anxious figure. Shy, awkward around girls, conflicted about religion and sex, and generally gave the impression of being a mother's boy. He always seemed to find it difficult to fit in. While most of us were Boston blue bloods, his family were furniture dealers from St. Louis. Although he had some family connections in Boston and belonged to various Harvard clubs, he always seemed to be on the outside looking in. At the time, we all thought he was a man of the very smallest importance. I don't think any of us had any idea what was in store for him.

After exchanging empty pleasantries about the weather and the yellow fog that had briefly enveloped the seaside town the previous night, I started to reminisce about our time at Harvard. The old professors we used to make fun of, our mutual friend Stetson who had been killed in the war, the exotic and aging Cambridge socialite we nicknamed "Lady A" who liked to invite us students to tea at her bric-a-brac laden home. I told him a little bit about myself. How I had gone into my father's publishing business, how I'd specialized in publishing poetry, and how I'd helped one of our classmates make quite a name for himself as a modernist poet.

At first, Prufrock was the reserved self that I remembered but after a couple of glasses of wine he started to open up. He told me about his life. The now famous life that we all thought we knew every detail of. He said he was fed up with it all. He was fed up with being a cultural icon. All those teas with cake and ices with women who wanted to talk about Michelangelo, those formulated phrases, those overwhelming questions. Women, always women—usually those arty types past their first, or second, bloom of youth—who couldn't get enough of him. They all wanted to be seen walking with him at dusk along a half-deserted street, or having dinner with him at an oyster restaurant and, above all, having a one-night stand at a hotel that, for some reason, always had to be a cheap one.

"Look" he said, and taking a handful of coffee spoons out of his pocket he threw them onto the bar. "I have to do this every time I go out and count the damn things as if I'm measuring out my life. I can't tell you how sick I am of it. I could just as well be performing conjuring tricks at a child's birthday party." In short, he said, he was starting to feel that he was a bit of a fool.

He summoned the bartender and ordered another bottle of wine. He was now quite animated and said he wanted to set the record straight on certain matters. There were things about him that had been completely misunderstood. For example, his interest in acting: an activity that provided some relief from the monotony of his career as a civil servant. He had joined an amateur dramatics club and particularly enjoyed Shakespeare. He'd always wanted to play Hamlet, but the director said he lacked the self-confidence to be a major stage presence and was cut out only for minor roles, like the wall in *A Midsummer Night's Dream*. On another occasion the company put on a production of Oscar Wilde's *Salome*. He'd wanted to play

John the Baptist opposite the company's Salome. He had been madly in love with her. And, to this day, he could still recall the light playing on the soft down on her forearms. But he never had the strength to force the moment to its crisis, that moment when he would tell her how he felt. Maybe if he'd been able to play John he could have told her, but the director wanted her for himself and took the role while he, Prufrock, ended up as a mere prison guard. In short, it was the life of a frustrated thespian.

He summoned the bartender again and this time asked for a glass of soda water that he promptly poured over his feet. He saw my look of surprise.

"Soda water's a great way to wash one's feet, you know. Especially to wash out the grains of sand caught between one's toes. It's a little trick I learned from a friend of mine, Mrs. Porter. She and her daughter often did it. Why, it's almost a poem: 'Mrs. Porter and her daughter, wash their feet in soda water.'" He giggled at his ridiculous ditty and said, "See, I'm a poet, and I didn't know it." At that point he burst into laughter, a thin, reedy laughter, and repeated his line, "See, I'm a poet, and I didn't know it."

This was clearly something he found enormously amusing. I laughed politely, but was deeply concerned. His silly little couplet about Mrs. Porter brought back memories of certain moments at Harvard when, as a somewhat reluctant drinker—whether we liked it or not, in those days we all had to get drunk—he would break out into vulgar, satirical verse. But was this little outburst more than just the wine talking? Was this the first sign of dementia or, far more worrying, was he straying dangerously off script into poetic territory where he didn't belong? However, I felt it was better to say nothing at this point and let him continue.

Just then, two beautiful young women in swimsuits walked past our seats at the bar. They were holding hands and could see us eyeing their firm breasts and shapely legs. They gave us contemptuous little smiles, and as we followed their gyrating hips and buttocks we could hear then laughing. Laughing at us, no doubt—two middle-aged men thinking middle-aged thoughts. I winked at Prufrock. He blushed and looked embarrassed.

"Have you ever wondered," he asked.

"Wonder about what? A threesome with a pair of lesbians?"

He looked shocked. "No, no. That is not it at all. That is not what I meant, at all."

"What then?"

"Have you ever wondered about being a woman? I mean, being changed into a woman. Say, for seven years, and then being changed back into a man," he asked.

"You mean like Tiresias?"

"Exactly. Think of all the things you could learn about men and women. How they love, how they hate, about sex. It's all about sex, you know."

There was clearly something he wanted to tell me, something about sex. I topped up his glass of wine and nodded encouragingly.

"How much do you remember about Lady A?" he asked.

"Not a lot. I only went to her place a couple of times. I do recall you were there on one of those occasions. I think Satterthwaite and Woodbridge lost their virginity with her, or so they claimed. After all, she was pretty old. But I do recall Stetson saying he thought she had taken a real fancy to you, but you were so clueless around women that you wouldn't have been aware of it."

"I was there more than once. In fact, I visited her many times. I was impressed by her cultured talk. Her carefully caught regrets of a mysterious past, her talk of Paris in the spring, how I should seize the opportunities of youth. I would escort her to Chopin recitals, and discuss current events I'd read about in the newspapers. But over time she became more and more demanding emotionally. Talking about how she feared ending up alone. How she wanted to do more than just serve tea to her friends. And how I must live life to the full, 'before it was too late.' And then, one October evening, she said things to me that I scarcely understood about a relationship between us that I didn't know existed. It all made me feel very nervous and I left immediately."

Prufrock looked uncomfortable, but I could tell he needed to tell me more. I smiled encouragingly. "What happened next?" I asked.

"Later that same evening, there was a knock at the door of my boarding house room, and there she was dressed in a long black coat. Almost a shroud or so it seemed. Her face was pale and her eyes looked slightly tearful. 'I am so sorry to come uninvited,' she said. 'But I had to see you. When we parted this afternoon, I sensed you were very uncomfortable when I told you that I had been wondering of late why we had not developed into friends. And that all our friends were sure our feelings would relate. I could tell by the way you looked and the way you hurried out of the door that my words had upset you. *Pour quoi, mon cheri?* As I watched you from my window walking away down the street, I could see your hands trembling as you lit a cigarette. I am so sorry if I upset or unsettled you in any way. I just wanted you to know how important your friendship is to me. That is why I am here, to tell you that.'

"Before I had a chance to say anything she swept into my room, tossed her coat onto a chair, and started inspecting my room and possessions with a critical eye. She picked up the photograph on the mantelpiece, 'Your mother, I assume.' She ran a finger along the edge of the dresser, 'Your land-lady should do a better job of dusting the furniture.' She picked up the open book on my desk. 'What are reading? *From Romance to Ritual* by a Jessie L. Weston, a woman writer, no less. Do you think women can be better writers than men? And what's this chapter, *The Fisher King*, about? Do tell me. I so love to hear you talk about clever things.'

"She then walked over to my window. 'Look, I can see across the street into the room opposite yours. I can see a young woman. Do you know who she is? She's laying out some food as though she's expecting a visitor.' I didn't want to tell her that I often spied on my neighbor and her visitors, and what they did.

"I went over to the window with the intention of closing the curtains but at that moment a man walked into the woman's room. We both stood at my window transfixed as though watching a play. After the couple finished their meal, apparently in near silence, the man got up from the table, pulled the woman up from her chair and put his hands on her breasts. She seemed indifferent to his actions. He then pushed her onto her divan and pulled up her skirt. We watched them have sex. It was all over very quickly, and then he left. And then, all she did was smooth her hair and put a record on the gramophone. It was as though it didn't mean anything to her, to either of them.

Yet watching this scene aroused strong sexual feelings in me. I then became aware that my visitor, my fellow voyeur, was gripping my arm very tightly. Her face was flushed and her eyes had a slightly wild look about them. Then, still gripping my arm, she dragged me towards my narrow bed, pushed me onto it and sat on top of me. She pulled her skirt up over her hips, unbuckled my belt, and rolled me over on top of her. 'Take me,' she said. It was a command. I had to obey, yet I didn't really know what to do. I was still a virgin. Her hands guided me and it was all over very quickly. She got off the bed and smoothed her dress and her hair. She looked very pleased with herself, practically victorious. 'There…' she said, and gave me a patronizing kiss on the cheek and left.

"I had finally lost my virginity, yet I felt that what had just happened was even more sordid than the scene we'd watched only minutes before. I felt as though I was in an emotional wasteland, and that feeling has never left me. None of the affairs I've had since then have satisfied me either emotionally or physically. I always felt like a voyeur watching myself commit a sordid act with a woman I was never attracted to. In the end it became safer to fall in love at a distance, and not say or do anything for fear of being disappointed."

What Prufrock had just told me was cultural dynamite. He had revealed that J. Alfred Prufrock had broken out of his poem and, in a secret life, had lived in other verses. If this became known the consequences would be seismic. Vast tracts of scholarship and literary criticism would be negated. Tenure decisions might have to be reversed. It could even have an impact on the sales of the poetry books my company was publishing. Generations of young men seeking emotional solace, or contriving moments of sincerity in the pursuit of intimacy, would no longer be able to say, "Let us go then, you and I..." The magic would no longer work if it was discovered that Prufrock had had another life.

We are all trapped in our own poems, trapped in the expectations others have of us, the expectations we have of ourselves. We are prisoners of the narratives we construct for ourselves—narratives that we tailor over time to suit our needs, or the needs of others. That is our destiny.

Prufrock, in his unique way, was no different. The Prufrock that the world knew was a middle-aged failure, a man who had failed to live, had failed to love. But then, to varying degrees, haven't we all? That is why we needed him so badly. He could express all our anxieties without us ever having to admit them for ourselves. And, like Prufrock, we also have our secret lives. And be they real or the product of our interior worlds, they are an essential part of who we are. But Prufrock was not allowed to have that other life. He had to stay in his poem. He was absolutely not allowed to break out of it. The rest of us can venture out of our narratives if we so wish, but he couldn't. That was his destiny. But by having that destiny, that eternal role of failure, timidity and weakness, he had succeeded beyond his wildest dreams and achieved an iconic status that the rest of us can only dream of. Perhaps, for the first time, I realized just how important he was to me. But more than that I knew it was imperative, absolutely imperative, that the world never knew what he had just told me. His confessions could not be allowed to disturb the universe. But how could I tell him this? How should I presume? How should I begin?

I told him what he had never been told before: that the world truly loved and needed him and everything about him. His bald spot; that his arms and legs were thin; that his coffee spoons were not the cheap party trick he now saw them as—rather they were the keys to the universe. I told him that in his unique way he had truly squeezed the universe into a ball, a ball that the rest of us could hold in our own hands and, in that way, make the universe more manageable. And only he, J. Alfred Prufrock, had ever been able to do that. I reassured him that his secret would always be safe with me and told him that, at all costs, he must go back to being the original Prufrock; that he must never again stray into those other poems; that the poem in which he felt imprisoned was the poem that had liberated the rest of us. I think my appeal worked. I could see his body relax, and for the first time in his life he looked happy.

"What should I do now?" he asked.

I looked up at the evening sky. He understood my gesture and gave a modest little smile. "Shall I say, I have gone at dusk…?"

"Yes, yes," I said, "That's exactly what you should say." He got up and shook my hand in a solemn farewell. I thought he was going to walk into the town—again, those certain half-deserted streets—but, instead, he walked off down the beach as though he knew exactly where he was headed, as though he already knew where his journey would end. As he receded into the distance I saw him pause, listening for something out at sea…the mermaids. I then knew that all would be well with the world again.

CINDERELLA

It's the same old story, a story that's been told a million times. One minute you're on top of the world—or should I say, you think you're on top of your particular world—and the next minute you come round in a hospital bed. However, in my case I can't tell my version of this age-old story. I've had a stroke and I can't speak. The only person I can tell my story to is myself. I'm trapped inside my head and, for now, there's no way out. And when one's a prisoner in this unique form of solitary confinement, introspection takes over. In a way, there's little else to do but indulge in a rigorous self-examination. An evaluation of the past, what might have been and what has been. The sort of thing that a sensible person, and I've always been a sensible person, does well to avoid. It's rather like going to the doctor for a checkup, but now one is checking up on oneself. One asks questions about how one is feeling, listens to one's heart, and subjects oneself to what feels like an emotional prostate exam—humiliating, painful, and probably necessary. Sometimes, one has to probe where it hurts.

Let's begin at the beginning. Right now, I'm in an intensive care unit and trying to take in what's going on around me. I can see a couple of white-coated figures, obviously doctors, and my brother. What's he doing here? One of the doctors asks if I can understand what he's saying. I nod and he starts explaining to my brother, rather than me, what happened. By now, I've been able to reconstruct some of that myself. I was at work—I'm the senior project manager at a big engineering company—and had been studying the project spreadsheets. It's a classified project, so I can't say what it's about other than it's worth a lot of money to my company. I'd been giving myself a headache resolving a critical design issue, and must have been glued to my computer screen for hours when suddenly the screen went blurry. All I can recall was feeling dizzy, getting up from my desk, my right side feeling numb, and...bang, I'm in the hospital. It appears that my office staff immediately recognized that I was having a stroke and, as I later learned, by using one of the company's security patrol cars—flashing lights and all—were able to rush me to a nearby hospital. It's difficult to follow everything the doctor is saying, but I hear phrases like "rapid intervention", "CT scan", "thromboembolic stroke", something about a drug called TPA. But what I do follow is the doctor saying that, thanks to the rapid intervention, the effects of the stroke should not be too severe, and that I'd been very lucky. I have to say—only to myself, of course—that as an engineer, I generally don't hold with the luck concept, in both engineering and in life. To me, it's more a matter of having the right design strategy. But, as I have learned to my cost, life doesn't always follow a rational design. That's certainly the case right now and I have to say that the concept of "very lucky" now sounds wonderful. I'm also trying to understand what the doctor means by "not too severe". As he continues to talk, it appears to mean that with the appropriate course of speech and physical therapy, I could be back to normal, or close to normal, quite quickly—by which he means a matter of months. I'm a normal kind of guy—almost boringly so— and if there'd been a time when I was younger when I'd wished that I hadn't been so normal, normal now sounds pretty damn good.

The doctor tells my brother that if all goes well, I will be out of ICU in a day or two and then moved to inpatient rehab for a while. He explains that the success of therapy depends a lot on the discipline and commitment of the patient. My brother grins and tells the doctor that I'm an engineer, a problem-solver and one of the most goal-oriented people he knows. The doctor smiles. I feel a tear trickle down the side of my cheek. To think, I could be a normal guy who'd just had a lucky break. It doesn't get much better than that.

The doctors leave and it's just my brother, Doug, and me. He sits down by the bed and fills in some other details. My brother and my son, Bruce, are listed, in that order, as my next-of-kin with my company's Human Resources department. That's one of the good things about working for a top engineering company: everything is run with unfailing efficiency. A member of HR accompanied me to the hospital and as soon as she'd had a preliminary report from the doctors she was on the phone with my brother. He's five years older than me. I can't claim that we're particularly close. He's a successful lawyer with some fancy firm in San Francisco and he has a fancy wife who works for another fancy law firm in San Francisco. They have pots of money and, if we're honest, we don't have a lot in common. We try to meet up once a year for a few days. That's just about enough time to exhaust all our family news and recognize that we've run out of things to say. But there's little I wouldn't do for him and, as his presence confirms today, I think he feels the same way about me—as long as it doesn't take up too much of his valuable, billable, time.

But maybe I'm being unfair. He's here now and wants to help. Doug tells me that he was able to track down Bruce, currently on a trip to New Zealand with his latest girlfriend. Bruce sends his love and will, of course, come home "if necessary"; and "tell dad not to worry about me." Believe me, I'm not going to. It all sounds just like Bruce. His laid-back act is his way of avoiding anything that might interfere with him enjoying himself. He may be my son but, man, he can be so self-absorbed at times. Gets that from his mother. And talk of the devil, Doug then tells me that he also contacted Bruce's mother—that's how we refer to my ex-wife, Chris. Apparently, she thanked Doug for letting her know and sends me her best wishes. Hmm…knowing

Chris and my brother's lawyerly way of expressing himself, this probably means that she said, "So, why are you bothering me with this?"

The next day, Jonas Pickering, my company's CEO, is in my room for a royal visit. He's trying to be cheerful and solemn at the same time. I've known him too long to be taken in. However, he's brought along his personal assistant, Allison. She's a rather beautiful young woman who brightens up the room. I'm pissed that she has to see me in such a reduced and haggard state. She's brought a huge bunch of flowers and a giant get-well card from my team. She holds it up for me to read. I'm touched. Jonas goes on at great length about how much the company owes me—indeed they do—and how all the company's resources are at my disposal to help in my recovery. Anything I want. I only have to ask. I suppose I could have tried to say "thank you", but don't feel up to trying and give what I hope looks like an appreciative nod. Internally, I'm laughing at the irony of Jonas's statement. Right now, I'm incapable of asking anyone for anything.

Jonas reassures me that thanks to my "heroic" efforts, the project is on track and now in the capable hands of the assistant project manager. The prototype will be finished on time and the demonstration for the Pentagon brass will go ahead as scheduled. Jonas wishes, ho-ho, that he could nominate me for a Purple Heart. Nothing would make him happier than for me to be present at the demonstration even if…oops, he's about to say "…even if you're in a wheelchair", but he just catches himself in time to say, again, that nothing would make him happier than for me to be present at the demonstration, period. Actually, that isn't quite true. What would make Jonas even happier than seeing me at the demonstration would be if the generals like what we've done and give the company another huge contract.

Jonas takes my right hand, which is still feeling numb, in both of his and gives me his best sincere look, tells me not to worry about a thing, and leaves. Allison stays behind for a moment. She moves the flowers to a better vantage point and writes down a phone number that my brother can use to contact her. I give her a left-handed thumbs-up. She then runs out of the room after her boss. As she leaves I find myself admiring her butt. Maybe there's hope for me yet.

It's easy for me to be uncharitable about Jonas but, until now, I haven't really had the time to dwell on my thoughts about him. But now I do. We go back a long way. We were at graduate school together, albeit in different degree programs. Most of our social contact was through the student engineering club, a rather meaningless body that he quickly became president of. Things like that were important to Jonas. What I do remember the most—or should I say, haven't forgotten—was the time when we were competitors for an engineering prize. My entry was a robotic device using the latest ideas in nonlinear control and his was a device for improving a chemical-plant process. There was no comparison in terms of technical sophistication—mine was far superior—but Jonas, then as now, was the consummate salesman and he won the prize. I'm not a vindictive person but I do have a long memory, and when he irritates me I recall that long-ago episode, as unimportant as it is now. We were hired by our company at about the same time; Jonas in the management track and me in the technical track. We both rose through the ranks rapidly but, Jonas being Jonas, it was inevitable that he'd end up as CEO and my boss. Even if I don't particularly like him, I recognize how good he is at his job. The Jonases of this world can be very useful. He brings in huge contracts and always gives me everything I need to complete a project. Even if there were times when I wanted to say, "Jonas, you're full of shit", I never did. And even if I wanted to now, perhaps out of frustration with my reduced state, aphasia prevents me from speaking my mind and ensures that our relationship remains reasonably cordial.

I admire the flowers Allison brought. I wish there'd be a reason for her to come back for another visit, but I can't think of one. More seriously, I think about what Jonas meant when he told me not to worry about a thing—a well-intentioned phrase with an ominous ring. I know Jonas. I'm sure that as soon as he heard about my stroke he had a meeting with HR to talk through all possible scenarios: from me making a sufficient recovery to resume my current job to the range of severance deals he could offer me. I could imagine Jonas conjuring up some meaningless position for me like Vice President for Community Outreach and

Education, a position that could then be phased out after a year or so with a nice early retirement package. I latch on to the doctor's prognosis of "not too severe" and imagine myself making a spectacular recovery. I imagine striding vigorously into Allison's office with a big bunch of flowers to thank her for her support during my recovery. When I let my mind wander too far, I can be a total idiot. I remind myself that I'm an engineer, a really good one, and now I have a huge problem to solve. I want to solve it. I can't wait for the therapy sessions to start.

The speech therapist introduces herself as Susan Ferguson. She's wearing large, heavy-framed glasses that make it difficult to see the details of her face. Her hair has a few streaks of grey. I'm guessing she's about my age—middle-aged, whatever that means these days. She tells me that to begin with we are going to test my ability to name things. Before we start the exercise she asks if I prefer to be called Robert or Bob. I manage to say something that I think sounds like Bob. She smiles. It's a really nice smile. She asks me to name the objects on the table we're sitting at: pen, mug, notepad, water-bottle. She then asks me to name some animals. Off I go and attempt cat, dog, rabbit, bear, lion, tiger, giraffe—Bruce went through a giraffe phase when he was five—and then I get ambitious and try to say orangutan. I've no idea how that actually sounded to Susan but I'm rewarded with a big smile. After asking me to answer a series of questions with a simple "yes" or "no", she asks me to write down my name and address. I need all four fingers and my thumb to hold the pen. Susan tells me that I've done very well and that she's looking forward to our next session.

At our next session, Susan describes a variety of exercises that she'll ask me to do. These include identifying famous people in photographs, describing simple domestic tasks, and recounting well-known children's stories. Susan emphasizes that it's important not to feel frustrated when I try to talk. At this stage of my recovery any combination of words and mime represents progress.

"OK, Bob, please tell me how you would make a peanut butter and jelly sandwich."

Personally, I can't stand peanut butter and jelly sandwiches, but when Bruce was a kid he liked me to make them for him. Those were the good old days when Bruce was impressed by his dad. A dad who could turn making a sandwich into a fun exercise in geometry. We would discuss whether we should cut the sandwich into two rectangles or four squares, or various combinations of triangles. It's easy to forget how important those little moments are, and now I do little else but try to remember them.

Today my sandwich making is more mime than words. I lay out two imaginary slices of bread, saying something that I think approximates "bread." I unscrew an imaginary jar of peanut butter and spread a little on each slice. That was a little engineering trick that Bruce liked—it stopped the jelly soaking into the bread. Now it's time for the jelly.

Then something weird happened. I said "ham" and laid an imaginary slice of ham on the imaginary peanut-buttered bread, and triumphantly said "ham sandwich". Susan didn't miss a beat. A big encouraging smile, "Good job, Bob, that's the most interesting sandwich I've had in a long time."

Susan then moves on to another exercise. Now she's showing me pictures of famous people and asking me if I recognize them: The Beatles, Marilyn Monroe, Tom Brady, Taylor Swift, President Obama. I do quite well and can just about articulate most of their names. More encouraging smiles from Susan. I really like her.

Susan may have liked my sandwich, but I didn't. When I got back to my room, I obsessed about it. I knew I'd gotten it wrong. I'm an engineer and I don't like making mistakes. Why did I say, "ham sandwich"? There had to be a reason. Then I get it. It was another of those little moments from yesteryear. My father's mother was English. She called jelly "jam". As a little kid I thought that was very funny and used to go round saying "jam, jam, jam." So jelly became jam, and jam became ham. I would like to explain my mistake to Susan but don't yet have the word power to do so. Maybe I'll be able to once I regain my speech sufficiently. That seems quite a long way off right now. But it's a goal. I like goals.

Susan usually starts our one-on-one sessions with the same basic exercises to measure my improvement. At our fifth session she shows me a picture of the Beatles and asks me which one in the photo is Mick Jagger. Is this a trick, or did she make a slip? She sees the puzzled look on my face and realizes her mistake. She sits back in her chair, takes off her glasses and laughs. As she laughs she twists a strand of hair behind her left ear. This is the first time I get a good look at her face…and there she is: that laugh, the twisting of the hair, the smile. It's her. It's Suz. Incredible. I want to say, "Suz, it's me, Zak. Don't you remember me?" But, ever the sensible person, I hold back. If nothing else, I know I don't have sufficient mastery of my speech to say it, let alone explain myself. And would she even recognize me after the best part of thirty years? Since my stroke, I've stopped shaving and am now wearing glasses instead of my usual contacts. I was surely unrecognizable. To her I must look like just another middle-aged patient: tired and slightly unkempt. That's not how I'd like her to see me. And what if I'm wrong? Then she'll think I'm nuts claiming that I'm someone called Zak calling her Suz. But I'm sure it's her.

At work, the name on my door is Dr. Robert Smith PhD. Most of the company employees address me as Dr. Smith. A PhD from MIT commands a lot of respect in my world. However, my team members call me Bob, as do my family and friends. Bob Smith—a name doesn't get much plainer than that. Some might even call it a boring name. In her more vitriolic moments as our marriage broke down, Chris would mock me as "boring Bob"—sometimes in front of our friends—and accuse me of approaching our marriage as though it was an engineering manual, of trying to fix things by a book that didn't exist. My attempts to be calm and rational when she was angry only seemed to enrage her more. In the years since our divorce, I've tried not to dwell on those bad days, but I sometimes wonder what would have happened if I hadn't been so calm and rational, had shouted back, had told her that she was self-absorbed, selfish and frigid. But, of course, being the way I was, the way I am, I never did.

However, there is a little more to my name. On official documents my full name is Robert Z. Smith. The Z is for Zacharias, after my great-grandfather who was a Presbyterian minister. I did not like my middle name when I was a kid and pretended that I didn't have one. When I went to college—the University of Oregon in my case—I wanted, like every other student, to create an identity for myself. To find something that would distinguish me from the pack, something that would make me seem more interesting than I really was. All those little things, those little acts of defiance, that we tried at that age: growing a beard, getting a tattoo, body piercings, wearing something flamboyant, smoking pot. A beard was the most I dared try and I soon gave up on that. However, the one thing I absolutely didn't want to be was plain old Bob. Suddenly, my middle name was a boon and I went around styling my self as "Zak". I was sure that my contemporaries would find a Zak Smith much more interesting than a Bob Smith.

I was a serious and ambitious student and didn't have much time to socialize. Of course I obsessed about girls, but as soon as I told them I was an engineer, the beautiful and interesting girls, the ones I fantasized about dating, would laugh and walk away. Or so it always seemed until one magical day in my senior year. I was at a party and found myself talking to one of those unobtainable girls. When I finally confessed to being an engineering major, I was shocked when she said, "You're just the guy I'm looking for." It turned out that she was a psychology student and having trouble understanding the basic statistics she needed for her senior thesis. Could I help her? And so began that romantic fantasy that no student days would be complete without.

Her name was Suz Zelinsky. I never knew if Suz was short for Susan or Suzanne, but her name, along with everything else about her, seemed exotic to me. We'd meet at the campus coffee shop once or twice a week for her "lessons" and there I was, Zak the engineer, out in public with one of the hottest girl on campus, and hoping that the curious would think we were an item. Of course we weren't and she was dating other guys on campus—cool guys, rich guys, handsome guys. She had a reputation for being promiscuous. On the one hand I was terribly jealous, and on the other I just hoped that one day she would be promiscuous with me. She seemed to like my company and sometimes we went to a movie or for a walk. She told me how nice it was to have a friend with whom she could have intelligent conversations and who wasn't hitting on her all the time. I was just like the brother she never had and that, of course, was the last thing I wanted to hear. But I was totally hooked. Her smile, her laugh, the way she would twist a strand of hair behind her left ear when she laughed. Everything about her.

By early spring I'd received an offer from MIT. That was a dream come true. But to complete the dream I had the idea that I could persuade Suz, who was also graduating, to come with me to Boston. My rational side told me that I was being a total idiot, but one's student days are the time when one can, and perhaps should, be that idiot.

I had it all planned. I chose a beautiful spring day to suggest that we go for a walk in a park near the campus. We would wander into one of the wooded areas where we could be alone. I would tell her that I loved her and that she should join me in Boston, and then we would go back to my room and make love. That was the plan.

As we wandered through the park we came to a fork in our path. "Left or right?" she asked, and then she marched off to the left. A few hundred feet along that fateful path we came across a stray dog sitting by a log. He was a mutt with an endearing, piratical look. His pose was so cute that he could have been auditioning for the lead in Lady and the Tramp. And that was the end of our romantic walk. Suz loved strays. For the rest of our walk, now with that dog in tow, all she talked about were the strays in her life: cats, dogs, sparrows, the homeless old man she would pass on her way to school and to whom she would give the cookie out of her lunch box. There was no going back to my room, no talking about our future together, no making love. It was off to the Humane Society to have our new friend checked out and by the evening it was the three of us sitting on my bed, and I had definitely come in last.

How I cursed that damned dog. Even though I hadn't declared my feelings, I felt as though I'd been rejected in favor of that mutt. It hurt, and for the remainder of that last semester I put some distance between us using the perfectly plausible excuse that I also had my own senior thesis to complete and finals to prepare for. We still stayed on friendly terms but I think Suz understood what was going on.

That was almost thirty years ago and practically forgotten until now. I wonder, as I had all those years ago, what would have happened if we'd taken the path to the right. If there hadn't been a stray dog to distract her, if I'd said my piece, if we'd gone back to my room, made love, promised to love each other forever and…who knows? But in truth I always knew that it would never be and our paths would diverge as soon we emerged from our collegiate cocoon. Like a moth, Suz would flirt with the flames while I would follow a path well-traveled. The reality was that we quickly lost touch after we graduated.

And now, here I am in rehab recovering from a stroke and certain that my speech therapist was that hopeless love of my student days. My brother had brought me my laptop and I searched the internet to see what I could find out about one Susan Ferguson CCC-SLP. I was able to find a CV and, yes, she had majored in psychology at Oregon at the same time I was there. Ferguson was probably her married name. I wondered how many times she had been married and why she wasn't wearing a wedding band. But she was definitely Suz. And now what should I do?

Despite my current speech difficulties, or perhaps because of them, I was determined to speak out, to say what I had wanted to say all those years ago, even if doing so would now serve no useful purpose. And it would probably make me look like a fool. But maybe it was time I indulged in that luxury. The idea of speaking up after all those years seemed rather reckless—an alien feeling for me, but I was rather enjoying it. It was a case of "If not now, when?" I was sure my great-grandfather Zacharias would have used that famous phrase in some of his sermons; but he would have almost certainly disapproved of my invocation of it now.

Even if one is going to be reckless, one still needs a plan or, rather, as we say in my world, a strategic plan. It all depended on how rapidly my speech would improve, and then finding the right way and opportunity to tell Susan who I was. The doctors were telling me that I was making excellent progress. It would still be a while before I could consider returning to work, on a part-time basis to start with, but I estimated that I could be articulate enough to say what I wanted to say within a matter of weeks. I was going to speech therapy sessions almost every day. Three one-on-one sessions per week with Susan, sometimes accompanied by a trainee called Belinda, and the rest of the time in group sessions with other therapists.

One of the standard assessment tests was for me to tell the story of Cinderella. My first few attempts at this were a struggle. I knew what I wanted to say, but finding the right words and stringing them together coherently was difficult and frustrating. The story became part of my plan and I would practice telling it out aloud. When I felt ready, I would volunteer to tell Susan the Cinderella story again. My plan was that when I got to the part where the prince sends his minister to find the girl who could wear the glass slipper I would modify the story. The minister would say that he was looking for a girl called Suz, a psychology major at the University of Oregon, who had had some statistics lessons in her senior year from an engineering student called Zak. That would be even more original than my peanut butter and ham sandwich. Like any good engineer, I analyzed all possible scenarios, their probability, and all the likely responses from Susan. And, of course, I had to have a repertoire of answers to anything she might say. If her response was a friendly but indifferent, "Bob, that's the most unusual Cinderella story I've ever heard," I would apologize for a mistaken identity. On the other hand, if her response were some variant of, "Oh my God, you're Zak," I would say…well, I wasn't quite sure what I would say. I just hoped it wouldn't sound too foolish. The other part of my plan was much simpler: I now went to the therapy sessions clean-shaven and wearing my contact lenses. If I looked long enough in the mirror I convinced myself that there was still some residue of how I looked in my student days, and maybe Susan/Suz would see that too.

After several more weeks of speech therapy I felt I was ready and waited for my next one-on-one session with Susan without Belinda being present. When what I thought would be that session arrived, I was surprised to see Belinda enter the room alone. She explained that Susan had been called away on urgent family business and that she, Belinda, would now be taking over all of Susan's patients. Belinda clearly had a prepared script. She said that Susan was sorry that she had to leave so abruptly and couldn't say goodbye to her patients in person. In fact, she had written each of us a note. Belinda produced a little stack of envelopes from her briefcase and gave me one. It was addressed to Bob Smith.

The note was typewritten. It was just a form letter, clearly the same for each patient. The only personal touch was the patient's handwritten name at the beginning and her initials at the end. It read:

Dear *Bob*,

As Belinda will have told you I am going on an extended family leave and will no longer be able to continue as your speech therapist. Belinda is one of my most outstanding trainees and you are in very good hands. I am sure you will continue to make excellent progress in your recovery.

With best wishes,

S.F.

Susan Ferguson CCC-SLP

So that was it. It was as though another stray dog—fate, in this case—had thwarted my plans, again. I was clearly doomed to be plain old Bob, boring Bob, Bob the engineer, the guy who never got to say what he really wanted to say. Just as I was stuffing the note back in the envelope, I noticed an extra, hand-written, line at the bottom of the page:

Zak, I do remember us! Very best, Suz.

COFFEE KARMA

The coffee shop has the cool ambience befitting serious coffee drinkers—a self-absorbed clientele on public display, their faces tinged with the silvery glow from their computer screens as they tap away. Posters and black-and-white photographs, some for sale, hang on bare brick walls illuminated by low intensity spotlights. A chalkboard on the wall behind the cashier lists the day's coffees with tasting notes: hints of citrus, maple and pecan, a long finish—and a choice of preparation methods.

Like all such establishments it has its regulars, including me. But before I tell you about them I need to tell you about Jared. He's the barista, the master of ceremonies. It's funny how people often look the part they play, or we think they do. If you were to ask me to draw up a description of a barista in a serious coffee shop like this, Jared would fit the bill perfectly. He has a wispy reddish beard, always wears a black T-shirt, a knitted wool cap, and a short, bead necklace he'd picked up while hiking in Nepal (or so he told me). Since coffee orders are placed with the cashier, opportunities for coffee talk with Jared are limited to the moment when you pick up your sacred beverage from the separate counter bordering his *sanctum sanctorum*—a mad scientist's laboratory of coffee-making equipment. Jared's "laboratory" includes a bright red, three head, espresso machine, an array of pour-over filters, a couple of gooseneck kettles for the pour-overs, and a selection of French presses of different sizes. There are two grinders, a scale for weighing coffee portions, a couple of timers, and a large thermometer ostentatiously standing ready in a beaker. God forbid that any of Jared's coffees were ever brewed with water hotter than 190F.

For the most part, Jared is too busy to talk but a carefully chosen opening gambit can sometimes draw out a few drops of java wisdom, rather like those first few drops of espresso that precede the stream of black liquor that fills your cup. My first attempt at starting a conversation was a failure. I'd noticed that when preparing pour-over coffees he, or his assistant, MeriAnne, would always pour the water from their gooseneck kettles with an anti-clockwise motion. When I asked him why it was always anti-clockwise he gave me a contemptuous look and said, "Because we're not in the southern hemisphere." However, on one quiet afternoon he opened up to a question I'd posed about Central American coffee beans. He told me about a trek he'd made through Central America during the coffee growing season and, in particular, his pilgrimage to the geisha growing estates in the Panamanian mountains. When I asked him how he thought the geisha coffees compared with the even more expensive Indonesian civet coffee he opined that the latter was "a load of crap". Fortunately, I passed the test by chuckling and giving an approving thumbs-up. After that we became buddies in the way that regular customers can be buddies with their barista. And a word of warning to anyone who wants to talk coffee with Jared: *never* ask him if he can prepare a flavored coffee for you.

I know the names and preferred brews of the shop regulars—information that's revealed when Jared summons them to collect their orders. When one of them changes their routine and orders, say, a French press instead of their usual cappuccino, I speculate on what might have motivated that change. Were they having a good day or a bad day? I won't bore you with a list of all the regulars, rather I'll just tell you about those who starred in today's dramatic events. There's the group of four older guys who meet here every Tuesday morning: Milt, George, Tom, and Avram. They're all in their late sixties or early seventies. It's not that I eavesdrop on their conversations but when I walk past their table I pick up snippets that, with a little creative interpolation, tell their stories. Milt, who always orders a cappuccino, is something of a hypochondriac. I say this because although he looks quite healthy, he often produces a pill bottle to show off his latest medication and complain about its cost. Milt also has quite a mouth on him and enjoys spicing up his comments with choice profanities. George and Avram enjoy showing their friends pictures on their phones. Judging by George's benign smile, and the fact that he has a wedding band, makes me think that he must be showing off pictures of his grandkids. Avram doesn't have a wedding band and judging by the winks he makes to his buddies as he scrolls through his pictures, one has to think he's into the online dating scene and may be trying his luck outside the senior circuit. Tom is the quietest and least demonstrative of the group. He has a bit of a limp and sometimes comes in with a cane. It's difficult to guess what his story might be. Today they've all ordered their usual drinks: cappuccino for Milt, medium latte for George, Americano for Avram, and a pour-over for Tom.

Now, who have we here? A newcomer. A young woman— I'm guessing mid-twenties—with a rather nondescript but discontented face. Her long blond hair looks unwashed, and she's wearing black tights, a white T-shirt, and a loose black sweater whose sleeves almost cover her hands. She's clutching a large cell phone. She places her order, finds herself a corner table and immediately starts looking at her phone. She's scrolling through her messages and doesn't look at all happy. Jared calls out "French press for Lucy," and Lucy and her beverage are revealed. I would bet a dollar that she spells her name with an "i". Once Luci returned to her table she stares at the coffee pot as though the settling coffee grounds contain the secrets of the universe. But before

I can continue with my speculations about Luci, there're some more newcomers to examine.

The guy who's just walked in looks out of place here. He's clean-shaven with a short, military-style haircut. His untucked, short-sleeved shirt reveals tattooed, muscular arms. We get athletic types in here but they're usually the skinnier variety—the running and cycling crowd. This guy looks more like a wrestler. I'm guessing he's in his early thirties. Maybe he's an off-duty cop. Within a few minutes Jared calls out, "Cortado for Kevin," and Kevin is revealed. He sits a few tables away from Luci and sneaks a sideways glance at her. Otherwise he just sits and stares at his coffee. At first I assumed Kevin and Luci were total strangers but then I notice that she's also taken a couple of quick glances at him. They look so incompatible that I don't think this can be an online dating rendezvous, but now I'm thinking there's something going on between them. But before I can continue with these speculations another newcomer shows up.

This one also looks out of place. I could see through the window overlooking the shop's parking lot that she came in a pickup truck—a rather grimy Ford F150. I'm guessing she's in her late fifties. Her grey hair is tied in a short ponytail, tight jeans enclosing beefy thighs and a zipped up, tight fitting, leather jacket. Looks more like a retired Hell's Angel than a regular at a coffee shop like this. What's she doing here? She spends a few minutes staring at the list of the day's offerings. I wonder what her choice will be? I also enjoy guessing customers' names before Jared reveals them. This one definitely looks like a Jolene to me.

But now my attention is drawn back to Luci. She's just poured a cup of her French press. She sips it and grimaces. Something's wrong. She picks up her mug and returns to the front counter. She pushes past Jolene and holds out the mug to the cashier.

"My coffee's a bit gritty."

"That's normal for the French press method. That slight grittiness is what enhances the coffee flavor. The grounds keep a little of the natural coffee oils in the brew. But if you like, we can make you another cup by another method," was the polite, smiling, response from Kimmie, the curly-haired cashier who's on the till today. Kimmie raises her eyebrows, deliberately, just a fraction.

"No. I don't want to be a nuisance. Perhaps you could just run this cup through a filter."

Kimmie turns to Jared, rolling her eyes, "Jared, please run this through a filter," and turning back to Luci, now with a forced smile, "I'll bring it to you as soon as it's ready."

"No, I'll wait here."

Luci stands belligerently in front of the counter and scrolls through messages on her cell phone. She seems oblivious to the fact that Jolene and two other customers, including Tom, are waiting to place their orders. Jared is really smart: he makes a show of pouring Luci's drink through a filter, but surreptitiously switches her coffee for a pour-over he's just made. Luci sips on her new beverage. "It's lukewarm, could you heat it up in the microwave."

Kimmie explains, with exaggerated politeness, that microwaving would take the coffee above the ideal drinking temperature of 180F degrees.

"I don't care, I want my coffee hot. I don't mean to be a nuisance."

"No, no, that's quite OK. Sometimes it's difficult to find exactly the right coffee experience to match one's mood."

"What do you mean? What's wrong with my mood?"

Jolene who until that moment had apparently been waiting patiently to place her order explodes: "Goddam it, just drink your fucking coffee and get out of my fucking way. I've been standing here for the last five minutes trying to place my order while you've been whining about your stupid drink." She steps up to the counter and confronts Luci. Any trace of sweetness in her face has transformed into vitriolic rage. "So you think you're having a hard day, girlie? Let me tell you what a hard day's really like," and she unzips her jacket revealing the butt of a large handgun stuck in her waistband.

Luci immediately starts screaming, "Don't shoot, don't shoot," and now everyone in the shop knows that a disaster is looming. Some are just frozen, a few duck beneath their tables, and others are fumbling with their cell phones. A couple of guys have jumped up on their chairs and start filming the scene as though it's just another piece of entertainment to post on social media.

Kimmie somehow manages to stay calm, "Ma'am, if you'd like to place your coffee order, Jared would be pleased to make it for you right away." Perhaps, for just a split a second, the confrontation might have been defused but Luci keeps screaming, and now right in Jolene's face. This is too much for Jolene who pulls the gun—it's a Glock—out of her waistband and brandishes it at Luci. "If you don't shut your fucking mouth, girlie, I'm going to blow your fucking head off. I swear to God I will." Luci screams again and Jolene fires at her, point blank. It's as though Luci's head exploded. There's a spray of blood and bone fragments, most of which hit Kimmie in the face. Luckily for Kimmie, she faints and collapses behind the counter out of harm's way. Jolene then sees that Jared is trying to dial a number on his phone—presumably 911—and she takes a shot at him. Fortunately she misses, but the bullet hits the espresso machine. It explodes. Now it's boiling water and metal fragments flying everywhere. Some of the fragments hit Jared in the face. He clutches his head in his hands covering his eyes, and I can see blood dripping through his fingers. He starts screaming, "I can't see, oh my God, I can't see."

Tom, dear old Tom, the quiet one who'd been standing behind Jolene to ask for a refill, suddenly grips his cane in both hands and takes a wild swing at Jolene. He only manages to hit her on the arm and she immediately fires at him. The bullet hits him in the shoulder and he falls to the floor. Milt jumps up from his chair and starts screaming at Jolene, "You crazy fucking bitch, you crazy fucking bitch" and then dives onto the floor next to Tom and grabs his hand. "I'm with you old buddy, I'm with you." The whole coffee shop is in state of bedlam. Customers are screaming and the explosion of the espresso machine has triggered off a fire alarm and water sprinklers.

The one person who seems completely calm is Kevin. He's been watching Jolene very closely over these last few bloody moments. He then jumps up from his chair, pulls a small revolver from the waistband at the back of his pants—so that's why his shirt was untucked—and adopts the classic two-handed gun-holding stance. He shouts to Jolene, "Police..." but before he could fire his gun Jolene lets off two rounds at him, hitting him in the chest. There's a huge spurt of blood and he crumples to the floor.

I've been sitting in my usual corner, practically invisible to Jolene. It's my turn to act. It's the moment I've been waiting for. In the backpack that holds my laptop and tablet, I also have 9mm SigSauer with a laser sight. Jolene is now in a frenzy letting off shots in all directions, but fortunately not hitting anyone, and not noticing me as I take aim. She sees the flicker of the red laser beam as it crosses her face. She knows what it is, and what's coming. Just for a millisecond our eyes lock and I see a look of hopelessness in her face. I fire. It's a perfect shot, straight through the forehead and she drops to the floor, dead.

Just at that point, the fire alarm and sprinklers turn off and the bedlam turns into a total and eerie silence as the customers realize what's happened. And then it's bedlam all over again. Someone must have managed to call the cops—there's a roar of police sirens and a swat team crashes through the shop's glass door creating a shower of glass splinters. They're shouting at everybody to drop to the floor with their hands clasped behind their heads. Talk about too much, too late. I quickly slip my gun back into my backpack and drop to the ground as instructed. A few minutes later, all the survivors who can walk trot out of the shop with their hands up. Kevin, who didn't lose consciousness after he was shot, and saw me take Jolene down, is carried out on a stretcher. He's talking to a couple of police officers. They're looking at me and nodding approvingly. One of the officers comes over to me, shakes my hand, and asks for a statement. Today I'm a hero.

So what happened? What caused a woman like Jolene, or whatever her name really was, to suddenly snap and wreak havoc, killing and traumatizing a group of innocent coffee drinkers? Maybe she'd just been fired from her job, or had her home foreclosed. Or maybe her drug-addicted daughter had stolen money from her, or maybe it was nothing more than a parking ticket. Or maybe it was nothing at all. We'll never know.

But then, there's something else you'll also want to know. Who am I, the guy who hangs out in that coffee shop all the time, carries a laser-sighted gun in her backpack and is quite the markswoman?

Well, I'm a graphic novelist. My genre is action/adventure, and my office is the coffee shop. It's not just Jared's coffee that I need for my work, it's the cast of customers who fuel my imagination. In fact, almost none of what I've just told you actually happened. Luci, Kevin and Jolene (her name, it turns out, was plain old Jane) really were in the shop, and Luci and Kevin really did order their respective French press and Cortado. There was no doubt that Luci was having a bad day and she did take her coffee back to Kimmie, the cashier, and there was a certain amount of eye-rolling between Kimmie and Jared. And Luci really did get in the way of Jolene/Jane placing her order, but only momentarily. But that was enough to trigger off my flight of fantasy. Each step of my imagined drama unfolded in the series of images I've just described, and I'm now sketching them out on my tablet. And, as you must realize, I can't resist drawing myself into my own stories. And as for the gun, I don't own one. Never have.

BELLE LETTRES: A NOVEL

Chapter 1. In which Miss Sophie Palmer receives a mysterious letter and writes about it to her friend Miss Amelia Taylor.

Dear Madam,

It is my high honor to send you this humble missive in order to introduce myself. Ever cognizant of the highest standards of personal and social propriety—values that I know you share—I feel it is only proper for me to address you as "Dear Madam" in this the first of what I pray will be a long and fruitful epistolary intercourse between us. Should my respectful approach meet with your approval it will be my greatest happiness to henceforth address you by your name—a name that I hold in the highest esteem.

As one of the most refined, if not the most refined, ornaments of our idyllic rural community whose delicate tread graces the village high street in the pursuit of her daily errands, and whose sylph-like presence adorns our country lanes on her rural perambulations, it would be impossible for a well-born gentleman such as myself not to be moved by a sense of admiration for your esteemed position in our county. Indeed it is difficult to imagine the existence of a member of your fair sex of greater pedigree, beauty, charm, elegance, and condescension.

I send you this humble expression of my heartfelt admiration and respect for your august personage in the fervent hope, dear madam, that you will respond to these inadequate words of mine and give some indication that you acknowledge my respectful greeting and expressions of admiration that, in the fullness of time, will lead to a more profound friendship between us.

I remain, ever respectfully,
Your Admirer

*   *   *

Dearest Amelia,

I have received a letter from a gentleman—for I can only assume he is a gentleman. But, dearest friend, as you can see from my copy of his letter that I enclose, he does not reveal his name! His words are elegant and his tone is respectful so he is surely a gentleman. But who can he be? One can only surmise that he is a member of our county and of good family, for he claims to know my name. Indeed, he says, "It will be my greatest happiness to henceforth address you by your name, a name that I hold in the highest esteem." He flatters me with reference to my delicate tread and sylph-like presence. While I do believe

I am deserving of such praise—for you, my dear Amelia, have also praised my deportment—I also note that he uses such terms with reference to my walking along the village high street and our country lanes. Does this mean that he has been following me and observing my every move, and his words are not those of gentleman but those of one with a forked tongue and evil intent? Or, perhaps, he is indeed a true gentleman, but one of such gentle spirit and shyness that he is hindered in his desire to reveal himself to me; and his words about my pedigree and beauty are those of an earnest admirer. And so, my dear Amelia, what should I do? Should I destroy his letter or show it to my worthy guardian? Or should I, perhaps, discreetly and within the strict bounds of propriety, encourage a further correspondence in the hope he will reveal himself and his true intentions? I am, as ever,

Your loving friend,
Sophie

*   *   *

Dearest Sophie,

How blessed I am to have a friend such as you who will confide in me all her secrets. I have read, and reread, your copy of the letter you received from your mysterious gentleman—for I, too, believe he is a gentleman—and I am not unimpressed by his honeyed prose. Indeed, dearest

Sophie, I cannot deny that if I were to receive such a letter I might not be averse to considering it in a favorable light. However, we all know that young gentlemen can be impetuous, impertinent and, in their eagerness to impress us members of the fairer sex, can sometimes fail to respect our need for delicacy of expression.

But, dearest friend, as much as society demands that we be demure, modest and refined we also have our needs—and this I can only confess to a friend as dear and close as you—the need to hear our suitors express their ardour, their passion—in the most refined terms, of course—so that we may know their true hearts.

So, dearest Sophie, my recommendation is not to burn the letter or show it to your revered guardian. Rather, you should encourage further intercourse. However, whoever he is, you must make it clear that you will brook no impertinence or inappropriate familiarity. Young gentlemen should be dealt with firmly! You may offer him the carrot of friendship but also the stick of propriety! I remain, as always,

Your dearest friend,
Amelia

* * *

Dear Sir,

While it is not my custom to reply to letters from one who does not have the courage to identify himself, I am making a special exception in your case. Your words of address lead me to believe that you are a gentleman who upholds high standards of propriety—values of the utmost importance to one of refined breeding such as myself, and values that have forever been impressed upon me by my guardian, a gentleman of unimpeachable integrity who is held in the highest esteem in our community. A fact that I am sure you must know, since you claim to know my name. He, Sir, is my protector and should I perceive the slightest hint of impertinence or inappropriate familiarity in any future letters from you, I will not hesitate to show him your missives and you—whoever you are—will have him to answer to! But should you wish to write to me again, and do so in a respectful manner, and on topics of an elevated spiritual nature, I would not be ill disposed to consider further communications from you.

I, Sir, unlike you, proudly sign my name,
Miss Sophie Palmer

Chapter 2. In which Sophie receives another letter and asks for Amelia's advice.

Dear Miss Palmer,

Would that I could summon up the courage to commence this epistle with the salutation "My Dear Miss Palmer" but, as one who has admired you from afar and fully recognizing your refined and delicate sensibilities, and impeccable reputation for propriety, I address you, ever correctly, as "Dear Miss Palmer". And so, Dear Miss Palmer, let me first state that my cup of happiness overflowed on receiving your letter indicating that you would not be averse to receiving further communications from your humble admirer. You cannot imagine the bliss that your stern directive engendered, and let me reassure you that all my words will aspire to the noblest sentiments and spiritual elevation. I am also fully cognizant of the fact that you may still not recognize the hand of this inadequate scribe who modestly introduced himself to you as Your Admirer. Yet I can assure you that I have basked—albeit at a most respectful distance—in the radiance of your fair countenance and, as surely as the sun coaxes a flower to blossom and a gentle Spring shower freshens the air, you have inspired me to strive for the necessary self-improvement of my soul so that, in time, you may come to consider me as your faithful servant in that most edifying of journeys—that noble quest for the meaning of life itself.

Do you recall yesterday's hunt—that quintessential expression of our finest rural traditions—and the Squire's most loyal hound whose long silken ears you stroked with you fair, gloved hand? Yes, that commendable canine was I! Do you recall his Lordship's noble steed whose glistening flanks you patted? Yes, that manifestation of equine excellence was I! I can assure you that my transmogrification into those quadrupedal forms whose pre-ordained roles in His Creation are to serve their bipedal masters is, of course, a statement of my most fervent desire to stand loyally by your side and serve your every need and, indeed, be your guide in seeking the ultimate truth. And, dear lady, let me assure you that I am most eminently qualified to perform this great task since my canine and equine proclivities are more than just metaphorical: for, indeed, I am a dog, I am a horse! Indeed, at that magical hour as night turns to dawn I may be seen by those of a kindred spirit gamboling along the hedgerows that border your worthy guardian's estate, vaulting the gates and pursuing the foxes. Thus, should you arise from your fair slumbers at that special hour and attune yourself to your anthropomorphic sensibilities you will see, in those not so distant fields that can be viewed from the window of your chamber of nocturnal repose, the author of these words in the pursuit of that perfection so necessary to lead you—or dare I say, us—along the path of enlightenment and eternal happiness.

Thus I remain your ever-respectful admirer,
Your Horse and Your Hound

*   *   *

Dearest Amelia,

He has written to me again! But, my dear Amelia, as you can see from my copy of his letter, I fear that he has not heeded my instructions to write only on elevated and spiritual matters. While it could be said that his initial remarks concerning the squire's hound and horse are not without a modicum of charm and evidence of a certain exuberance on his part, I feel that his references to my caressing those creatures' anatomical parts to be indelicate to say the least. While I might have been willing to excuse his observation of my stroking the ears of the squire's hound, his reference to my patting the horse's glistening flanks is quite unacceptable. But his statements about my guardian's estate and—here I almost swooned—his reference to my chamber of nocturnal repose is, as I am sure you will agree, the most extreme vulgarity and impertinence! That he somehow knows that I can view the fields from my bedroom window is most frightening and, I fear, puts my honour at risk. This is no gentleman to be sure! What a truly impudent and dishonorable young man!

And so, my dearest Amelia, surely I should I now command him to cease any further correspondence and have this nonsense finished with once and for all? I eagerly await you reply and advice. As always,

Your loving friend,
Sophie

*   *   *

Dearest Sophie,

I fear you may have over-reacted to <u>your</u> young gentleman's letter—for he is surely now your young gentleman!
For my part, I thought his references to the squire's horse
and hound to be rather charming and full of an exuberance
that is quite diverting, and certainly far more entertaining
than the dreary intercourse we have to tolerate from the
young men with whom we are permitted to be acquainted.
And, I think, you should not let your sense of delicacy be
overly offended by his reference to your touching certain
anatomical parts of those noble animals. To me, my dear
Sophie, they were an expression of the strong feelings that
you have aroused in him. Indeed, and do not think me to
be in any way jealous of you, I would be flattered to have
received such a letter expressing those sentiments.

However, I do agree with you that his reference to your
chamber of nocturnal repose is far too forward for a gentleman of refined breeding. But here again, dear Sophie, do
not be too hasty in your judgment of him. For, I believe,
you are now embarked on a great adventure! An adventure
of the sort we have hitherto only imagined for ourselves. I
do not believe he is a Montoni or a Count Morano; rather
he could be your Valancourt—but, I hope, a wealthy one!
Nonetheless, he should not be encouraged to think that
such forwardness will not go unpunished. And so, dear
Sophie, you should give him a strong reprimand and remind

him of your revered guardian's standing in the county. I remain, as always,

Your dearest friend,
Amelia

*   *   *

Dear Sir,

You, Sir, are not the gentleman you would have me believe you are! Despite my strict instructions that you only write to me on elevated matters of the soul, you proceeded to write to me in a most scandalous and indecent manner. How, Sir, could you dare to refer to my chamber of nocturnal repose! If my guardian were to see your letter his wrath would know no bounds and your punishment would be severe. You, Sir, would be disgraced.

However, despite your transgression, I am not without mercy and I found it in my heart to look for some faint glimmers of goodness in your letter. It is possible that I was not totally unmoved by your reference to the squire's horse and hound—two noble creatures to be sure. However, your reference to my caressing the ears of that fine hound and, in particular, my patting the flanks of that noble horse was most indelicate. Be warned, Sir, that a lady of my refinement and good breeding will not countenance such familiarity. Although I am very much of the opinion that I should cut off all further correspondence with you, I am willing to give you one last chance to redeem yourself.

I remain, Sir,
Miss Sophie Palmer

Chapter 3. In which Sophie receives a third letter and is greatly distressed.

My Dear Miss Palmer,

I have abandoned all caution to the wind and now address you as "My Dear Miss Palmer"—an act of salutatory daring on my part that, I pray, you will recognize as the greeting of one who holds you in the highest and purest esteem.

I realize that my previous epistle, signed by your faithful Horse and Hound, might have aroused some elements of maidenly concern on your part, but I can assure you that my references to your caresses of my canine ears and patting of my equine flanks were simply an exuberant and, dare I say it, poetic attempt to express in metaphorical terms my heartfelt admiration for your generosity of tender feelings towards God's creatures of which I am a most humble, if not the humblest, one.

I also fear that my reference to the distance between the window of your chamber of nocturnal repose and the hedgerows where your faithful Horse and Hound gambols at dawn might have caused you to question the presumption and motives of that innocent act of rural cartography. Let me assure you, My Dear Miss Palmer, that you should have no anxieties or concerns with regard to the purity of my feelings and admiration for you. Indeed, in order to dispel any doubts and, in accordance with your commands, I will now open my heart to you with regard to spiritual matters and express how the centrality and sanctity of God's word guides me; and how following our Maker's commandments and the observance of those religious duties that glorify his Name will make me a worthy companion on your life's journey. And where better place to start than in our village church? An edifice at once both humble and infinitely grand, a sturdy monument whose foundations date back to days of yore, a testament to our very way of life, the very Jerusalem of our green and pleasant lands.

At last Sunday's service at which it was my privilege to attend and observe your devotions, I could not help but ponder on the profundity of the rituals, and the role that even the simplest of our church's furnishings play in our service—not only in glorifying His name but also in serving the corporal needs of His followers. Take, for example, the modest pew. To some it is a mere convenience: a seat for—dare I say it—the human seat. But it is so much more! Think of that labour of love performed by some skilled and humble craftsman of yesteryear as he carved and assembled the pew in full knowledge of the sacred purpose it serves. Run your hands—those delicate hands that only recently stroked the ears of your faithful Hound—over its hard surface, a surface that has been worn smooth by countless generations of worshippers. As you sit on that pew listening to the ministrations of our worthy pastor feel its firmness as it supports you—as would the back of your worthy Horse should you deign to mount him. But even more, dear lady, consider the sacred communion wafer—an item so small and light yet, in truth, one that carries the entire weight of the world for our sins. I could not help but observe, as you took Holy Communion, the delicacy with which you parted your cherry lips—so slightly moist and glistening in the pastel tinted light of our chapel—to accept that holy offering. Indeed, as I witnessed your beauty, your devotion and, dare I say it, your passion I could not but think...but no, I have already said too much! But rest assured, My Dear Miss Palmer, that my discourse on these artefacts of worship is not the idle musing of a verbose dilettante; rather it is the most heartfelt expression of my desire to assist you in your spiritual journey. For I am that pew upon which you sit, I am that wafer that passes your lips...

Once again, I pray that my outpouring of unalloyed admiration for your beauty of both body and soul does not, in any way, offend your sense of propriety.

Thus I remain your ever-respectful and devoted admirer,
Your Pew and Your Wafer

* * *

Dearest Amelia,

I have received another letter from him! When I started to read it I was, at first, quite pleased: his expressions of contrition for his unseemly language and thoughts in his previous letter were, I thought, elegantly expressed, and his religious sentiments appeared to be sincere. But, dearest Amelia, when I read on and saw that he, who ever he is, has been watching me in church, I was shocked and very frightened. He has been following me and spying on me everywhere! And, as you can see from the copy I have made for you, his indecency and gross familiarity continues unabated! It was bad enough that he talked about my stroking the ears of the squire's hound, but now he wants me to stroke the pew on which I sit! And even more scandalous was the implication that he has been considering a most private part of my anatomy, one that I cannot even bring myself to name. And as to what he said about my taking of the Communion Wafer, I consider it to be most disgusting and reprehensible. It was sacrilegious in the extreme!

It is now clear that not only is he not a gentleman but, I fear, he is also a madman. For who else would spy on a young lady in church, and sign himself "Your Pew and Your Wafer"?

Dearest Amelia, his letters are more than most vexing. They and the knowledge that he is spying on me everywhere are putting me in a most terrible state of nervous agitation.

This is no longer an adventure—it is turning into a nightmare!! What should I do?

Your loving and now anxious friend,
Sophie

*   *   *

Dearest Sophie,

Like you, I was, at first, not unimpressed by your young gentleman's letter (for I still believe he is a gentleman) but I certainly understand how distressed you were to read what he wrote about your attendance at church. But, I wonder, did you really feel that his thoughts on your taking the Communion Wafer were truly sacrilegious? Were you not in the slightest degree excited by the way he observed your parted lips? For, dear Sophie, your sweet mouth is one of the finest features of your facial physiognomy, as you yourself have observed on more than one occasion.

While you have every reason to fear that he is following you, I do not think he is a madman. Rather, I think, he is a deeply troubled soul tormented by his love for you. And if this is so, it is not threats of your guardian's wrath that will cure him of his epistolary folly but rather he is in need of some gentle caresses of a spiritual nature to soothe him. Surely, dear Sophie, you can find it in your generous and Christian heart to give him some kind words that will calm his troubled soul. So, dearest friend, give him one more chance. I am, forever,

Your loving and best friend,
Amelia

* * *

Dear Sir,

I was greatly distressed...no, Sir, I was truly shocked, by your most recent letter. It is clear that you have been following me and spying on me everywhere—even in church! Sir, have you no decency! And the things you said! They were grossly familiar, indecent, and impudent, and showed—despite your earlier claims—a complete disregard for any sense of propriety.

I believe a more sensible and less forgiving person than myself would, without hesitation, have ceased this correspondence long ago and destroyed your letters. But, Sir, we are taught to help those in need; for I do believe you are troubled and, perhaps, your better judgment has been clouded by the intense feelings you have for me. So, Sir, I am willing to forgive your most recent and extreme epistolary transgressions in the hope that you will regain your composure. I am willing, for the very last time, to give you the chance to write to me again—but only on the absolute condition that you refrain from any further indelicate and vulgar language, and indecent sentiments. I remain, Sir,

Your most disapproving correspondent,
Miss Sophie Palmer

Chapter 4. In which Sophie receives a most frightening letter.

My Dear Sophie,

Oh woe is me that I should have said, in the exuberance of my admiration and tender, but purest, feelings for you, anything that offended your sense of propriety. Please forgive me! And such is my ardour I must now presume to address you by your Christian name—and could there be any finer appellation for you than Sophie? Sophie, the Greek word for wisdom. Sophie, mother of Faith, Hope, and Charity: three virgin martyrs to their faith. And so, My Dear Sophie, please pardon this appellatory presumption on the part of your humble admirer—one who is now, as a consequence of our intimate correspondence, your truest friend.

Yet I fear that my previous missives, from your faithful Horse and Hound and from your Pew and Wafer, have failed to adequately express the extent to which I am able to serve your needs—needs that would be my greatest honour and highest aspiration to minister. Pray consider your chamber of nocturnal repose: that sanctuary of physical and spiritual requiescence, a veritable Garden of Eden of peace, security and comfort where, in the words of the Immortal Bard, "Golden sleep doth reign." Thus, having knelt by your bed to say your prayers and climbed into that luxuriant cradle of

169

nocturnal rest, embraced by silken sheets, you descend into peaceful slumber and embark on journeys of the sweetest dreams befitting one of such purity of spirit. Would that you dream of your faithful Horse and Hound, of your Pew and your Wafer! But fear not, you are not alone in your nocturnal peregrinations, for I am the pillow that cradles your silken tresses and caresses your fair cheeks. For surely, to again quote words of The Bard himself, you are "…such stuff as dreams are made on."

Night ends its gentle embrace and dawn opens its heavenly doors. The winged angels of our Lord's creation, the blackbird, the robin, and the chaffinch serenade you with their melodious matins, and the distant cock does crow, "Awake sweet Sophie, a new day begins!" As you sit at your dressing table and look in the mirror while you brush your auburn hair, you contemplate—with the greatest modesty, of course—your beauty. But cast aside your modesty for a moment, My Dear Sophie, for I am your mirror that proclaims your beauty; the reflection that you see is my image of you. Thus, as your pillow and your mirror, I am always there to watch over you in your chamber of nocturnal repose—that sacred sanctuary where you disrobe, and sleep, and dream.

Thus I remain your ever-respectful and devoted admirer, Your Pillow and Your Mirror

* * *

Dearest Amelia,

He is truly a madman! I took your advice, my dear
Amelia, and held out the hand of Christian charity and
understanding in the hope that he would regain his composure and write to me in more measured tones—in ways
that befits a gentleman to write to a lady. But look at what he
has written to me! He has invaded my chamber of nocturnal
repose! I am now so frightened that I am barricading my
bedroom door at night for fear that he might break into my
guardian's estate and force entry into my room, or worse.

I am at my wits' end and do not know what to do. I
know that I must now go to my guardian for protection,
but I fear he will be very angry with me for having allowed
this immoral correspondence to continue for so long. And,
dearest friend, your own letters of wise counsel to me will
also implicate you in this affair. It could mean disgrace
for us both!

Your dearest and frightened friend,
Sophie

Chapter 5. In which all is revealed.

Dearest Amelia,

I do not know where to start—for today has surely been
the most dramatic day of my life! After having written to
you this morning I was in such a state of distraction that I
foolishly took into our library some of the letters from my

deranged admirer, and some of your letters as well. And, even more foolishly, I left them unattended—and my guardian found them! They put him into the most frightful rage. He told me that any man, young or old, who would write such indecent and impertinent letters to me deserved to be horsewhipped. Indeed, he would personally horsewhip the scoundrel from here to London and back. He also saw that I had involved you, my dear Amelia—the daughter of his old comrade-in-arms, Sir Edmund Taylor—in what he termed this most sordid affair. He demanded that I reveal, at once, the name of the reprobate who has been writing these obscenities to me.

Oh, dear Amelia, what could I do? I threw myself on his mercy and told him that I had written all of those letters myself, and that they were all part of a silly game we were playing. My dear guardian looked at me in amazement and I thought that my wicked deception would result in me being banished from his house forever! But no! He laughed and embraced me, and told me that I was a silly girl just like my late mother—his beloved younger sister—whose head had always been full of romantic nonsense. He said that Mrs. Radcliffe had a lot to answer for, putting foolish ideas into the heads of young girls. But then he became quite serious and said that if any man, whoever he might be, wrote to me like that he would horsewhip him. Indeed, he and Sir Edmund together would horsewhip him to London and back. He did go on so about horsewhipping! And then he said that since I was now seventeen, it was high time that I married instead of wasting my time on girlish games and silly daydreams. Indeed, he would talk to Lady Morgan this very week about finding a suitable match for me.

To think, dear Amelia, that I am going to be married! I would very much like to be married, but I think seventeen is too young. I would so much like to have more experience of the world and young gentlemen before I marry. I think I would like to be married when I am eighteen when I am as old and wise as you. And, certainly, if I wait till I am much older than eighteen people will think of me as an old maid. But rest assured, dearest Amelia, that I will subject my chosen suitors to the most rigorous examinations when they make love to me, and will rely on you for your wise counsel. Oh, what a day!

Your dearest and happiest friend,
Sophie

Chapter 6. In which Sophie is put in a state of terror.

My Dearest Sophie,

I trust that my missives have convinced you of my inestimable regard for you, and the purity of my feelings towards you. Indeed, having now expressed myself to you as Your Horse and Your Hound, Your Pew and Your Wafer, and Your Pillow and Your Mirror, I feel that our epistolary intercourse has reached a natural climax and that the hour has come to consummate our spiritual communion—not with a continuation of my clumsy epistles but, rather, with a meeting between our two personages. Yes, a meeting! The moment has come when it will be my high honour to address you directly in the flesh, and for you to finally set eyes on your humble admirer in the hope that you will not find his appearance to be totally disagreeable—if not worthy of the thoughtful prose with which he has addressed you.

Indeed, I tremble at the thought of being able to raise my hat to you and kiss your gloved hand in direct but most respectful greetings. Perhaps it will be on a deserted leafy lane as you wend your way home on a solitary perambulation at gloaming time as the crows fly over the fields into the distant golden sunset—a sunset as golden as your beauty. Oh, My Dearest Sophie, our moment has come! I cannot wait any longer. Till we meet!

Thus I remain your ever-respectful and devoted admirer, The One Who Awaits You

* * *

Dearest Amelia,

I am going mad. As you can see he has written to me again! I am now in a state of terror, for whoever this monster is—he who knows my every move and thought—he is lying in wait for me! It was bad enough needing to barricade my bedroom door, but now I am too terrified to leave the house, let alone walk around my guardian's estate—even when protected by our loyal wolfhound, Brutus—for fear that this depraved madman will ambush me and do me the most terrible violence. But what shall I do? For having told my guardian that the man who wrote those letters does not exist, I cannot now tell him that he does! Who will protect me? What should I do? Dearest Amelia, pray help me! I am, until the end,

Your dearest and most terrified friend,
Sophie

STEVE

If you asked Steve's coworkers what he looked like the replies would vary. Most would say he was of medium build and medium height. Some would say he had brown hair, and others would say it was black. A few coworkers thought he had a small mustache and nobody could say for sure whether he wore glasses or not. But, without fail, he was at the office every day busily running errands and working the copier, and quick to say, "Have a nice day" and "Have a good one". But apart from some sports talk by the water cooler he didn't say a lot and generally kept to himself.

Although Steve was quite happy to blend in with the office furniture, he sometimes wondered if his coworkers noticed him at all or, more interestingly, if they thought he had a big secret. He wondered if they thought he was another Norman Bates with a taxidermy collection in his cellar, or perhaps he was a Mafia hit man turned informant who was in a FBI witness protection program. Steve liked the idea that there could be such speculations about him because being the subject of people's curiosity would mean that he was a somebody and not a nobody.

In fact, Steve's big secret was that he didn't have a secret. Well, not the sort of secret he thought people would find interesting. The truth was that for most of his life he had tried to be a nobody. For that was how he had survived. After a childhood spent in foster homes he'd learned the way to stay out of trouble and avoid being cursed at, and sometimes beaten, was to make himself as small and quiet and invisible as possible. That was how he avoided the disappointment that always came with hoping people would like him and want to be his friend. He got through high school without ever really being noticed, and after a few small jobs here and there life was now pretty good. A steady office job that paid the rent, a few coworkers with whom he could make small-talk about sports, and a pretty receptionist who would always give him a nice smile.

Life had taught him that it wasn't worth wondering if she actually liked him—that would only lead to disappointment. But a nice smile was always welcome and sometimes he would take it home with him; but he was always careful to leave it at his door before locking himself in for the night. Yes, his life as a nobody was good, and without the complications that came with trying to connect with other people. But lately he had started to wonder if life could actually be better. Was it possible for the nobody he assumed he was to become the somebody he would like to be? Deep down he believed he would always be a nobody, but at least he could try.

To become that somebody required a plan. The first thing to do was to start being noticed, but in the right sort of way. Sure, he could show up to work in a clown's suit—that would certainly get him noticed, probably laughed at, and almost certainly fired. Rather, the idea was to become noticed in a stealthy sort of way so that nobody would notice that he hadn't been noticed before. And then, without anybody realizing it, it would no longer be, "Steve, could you run down to the deli and pick up the sandwiches," but "Do you want anything from the deli, Steve?" or "Steve, I'd really value your opinion on this..." Steve didn't mind picking up the sandwiches—everybody at the office assumed that's what he was there to do—and at the deli, at least, he was a somebody. "Hi Steve, here to pick up the sandwiches?" and while he was gathering up his load, "What did you think of the game last night, Steve?" and whether it was football, baseball, basketball, hockey, or even bowling, he would have something to say. At the deli he was somebody: Steve the sports-buff. He liked that and worried that if he became the new Steve, the somebody Steve, the Steve who no longer had to go to the deli to fetch the sandwiches, he would miss his visits there and talking to Frank, the owner, about the game. And as for what, one day, he would be asked his opinion on, he wasn't quite sure.

The first step towards being noticed was to change his appearance. The coworkers who thought he had a small mustache were wrong, he didn't. There'd be no doubt about how he looked if he had a beard. Beards were definitely in these days. There was James Harden with his big bushy beard, and LeBron often had one too. But he wasn't James or LeBron, let alone Aaron Rodgers or Bryce Harper. He thought a big bushy beard would make him look like a hobbit. The guys in the commercials for cologne and sports cars usually had a few days growth of carefully manicured stubble; and they often wore sleek, metal-framed glasses as well. Yes, that would be his look. It was really cool.

The stubble would just show up on his face without anyone really noticing. The coworkers who thought he wore glasses were also wrong, he didn't. He could get himself glasses with plain lenses, maybe even a slight tint. To begin with, he could just put them on occasionally until nobody would notice that he was wearing them most of the time. And then, without anybody realizing it, it would no longer be "Have a nice day, Steve", but "Looking good, Steve." Maybe it would be Cynthia, the receptionist, who'd start saying it first. But, if he was honest with himself, it wouldn't be "Looking good, Steve" if he was still wearing his brown pants, beige shirt and red tie most of the time. His last foster mom was very keen on brown. She said it was a sensible color that didn't show the dirt. He didn't have a lot of money for clothes and had never given much thought to how he dressed, but now it was time to change. The people at his office who met with clients wore suits or blazers, but he knew his co-workers would laugh at him, the office boy, if he showed up in a suit. The guys with the sports cars, the colognes, and the perfectly trimmed three-day beards often wore a slim-cut sport coat over a dark crewneck. He reckoned he could change into that look without anybody really noticing. He'd first trade in his brown pants for black ones, and then his beige shirt for a blue one. By the time it was fall he could start wearing a sport coat. If Marty said, "What's with the coat, Steve?" he could say, "Fall, Marty." It would then be a small step to go from the shirt to the crewneck. And once that was achieved, nobody would notice that the black pants had been replaced by black jeans. And then it really would be, "Looking good, Steve." By then, those of his coworkers who couldn't remember if he'd ever had a mustache or wore glasses, wouldn't remember the time that he didn't look sharp. They'd assume that he'd always looked sharp, and that he was the guy to ask for his opinion.

The clothes and glasses were items he could afford. That still left the choice of cologne. Steve did a lot of research online about men's fragrances and the importance women attached to a man's smell. It was all about the pheromones. Some of the "specially for men" products being offered online made amazing claims. Some would have women falling at your feet after just a couple of whiffs, others would give you an "alpha/elevated status" that would make people think highly of you, and the most expensive products would do both for you. But first things first: he'd start off in the mall where they were always giving out free cologne samples. The beautifully made-up girls at the fragrance counters would probably ignore him if he showed up wearing his brown pants and beige shirt, so he'd use these trips to practice wearing his new outfit. He was sure this would result in lots of free samples, and he could also practice his small talk by asking them for their opinion on which scent suited him best. Yes, he was sure he could find just the right cologne so that Cynthia would say, "Love your aftershave, Steve."

The new Steve, the looking-good Steve, the Steve whose opinion people sought would, of course, be the sort of Steve that people, especially women, would want to be around. And this was his greatest concern. He didn't have any friends and he didn't have a girlfriend. At the annual office party he would always show up by himself, making the excuse that his girlfriend couldn't come for some reason or another. He knew that these excuses were wearing a bit thin, and he worried that this was leading to speculation that he might be gay. In fact, he'd never had a girlfriend. In fact, he was still a virgin. This was his biggest source of shame and anxiety. How could a man, any man, his age still be a virgin? He'd read online that there were well over a million men in the US between twenty and forty who were virgins, and in some Asian countries the percentage was higher. Apparently, some men chose to be virgins for religious reasons, but the main reason was extreme shyness and anxiety. Steve was very shy, but more than that he was frightened of sex. He could never clear his head of the cries he had heard, night after night, from the bedroom of the foster parents he had had when he was twelve. He had tried to get over his phobia by binging on porn movies. There were no shortage of cries—a different sort—in those movies, but that didn't make him feel any better. And the porn stars never had the bruises he would sometimes see on his foster mother's arms and neck. He knew that there were also porn movies that showed women being beaten or tortured, but he couldn't bring himself to watch them. He didn't need to.

When Steve got home from work he'd usually have a microwave dinner and a beer while watching ESPN. After dinner, he'd often play his sports bar game. He'd pretend that he was sitting at a bar next to a famous athlete and they would strike up a conversation. He'd sit at his small dining table and by careful positioning a couple of lamps would project two separate shadows of himself on the wall. In this way he could act out the conversation. As much as he would like to be chatting with the all-time greats like Michael Jordan or Tom Brady, he would set his sights a little lower and talk to good guys like Mike Trout and J.J. Watt. Sometimes he would be an ESPN presenter and do interviews with coaches like Mike Tomlin and Steve Kerr. He'd read somewhere that living in the dark meant living without a shadow, so by creating two of them he reassured himself that he wasn't living totally in the dark. And sometimes he'd play a different game: instead of being Steve the sports journalist he'd be the somebody Steve, and the other shadow would be a girl—a girl who he'd just met at the bar and struck up a conversation with.

The previous tenant of his rental apartment had left behind a queen-sized bed frame. Steve kept it and bought himself a recycled queen-sized mattress. Maybe, by having the big bed he would, one day, find someone to share it with. And like the shadows on his living room wall he often went to bed with an imaginary partner—someone much warmer and more beautiful than he could ever hope to meet.

When he was in his late teens, Steve had spent some Thanksgivings with the family of his social worker, Mrs. Felice. Since then he usually went to Denny's by himself for their Thanksgiving Special. Then, out of the blue, Mrs. Felice contacted him and invited him for Thanksgiving. She gave him a big hug when he arrived, told him that he was looking "all grown up", and asked if he had a girlfriend—to which he mumbled an ambiguous reply. Mrs. Felice told Steve that she no longer worked for Social Services and was now working for the city's housing department. Otherwise, she was as he remembered her. A solid, friendly, and reassuring figure. Her two daughters, Kim and Tina, who were about the same age as Steve, were also there. They had changed a lot. Kim was at nursing school and Tina was there with a baby. Also present was Tina's boyfriend, Gary. However, the main difference from those previous Thanksgiving dinners was that the surly and hard-drinking Mr. Felice was no longer present. There was much less tension around the table than Steve remembered from before; everybody was relaxed, friendly, and interested in what Steve had to say about sports. That evening, Steve felt something he scarcely knew—a sense of family. When he left there were more hugs and Mrs. Felice, who insisted that he now call her Eva, told him not to be a stranger. When he got home he didn't leave her hugs at his apartment door. He took them inside and then to bed. Those were the only hugs he had had in more years than he could remember.

Steve was now wearing his new look to work. He was sure that Cynthia had noticed the change, although when she smiled at him he often had the feeling that she was trying to suppress a giggle. But one day she really did say, "You're looking good, Steve." Marty was his usual pain-in-the-butt self and would rib him about his jacket and glasses, and cologne. "What's with the new look, Steve?" "What's with the glasses, Steve?" "You stink like a fruit cake, Steve." But those remarks stopped when Marty showed up after his vacation sporting a wispy beard.

Some of the guys in the office had a regular TGIF at a nearby bar. A few of them were Steve's sports-talk coworkers and he sometimes joined them. But apart from the sports talk he always felt like the odd man out. They all seemed to have far more interesting lives than he did. They had wives or girlfriends—one of them bragged about having both a wife and a girlfriend—and they always had something to talk about, to argue about. He certainly couldn't tell them about his recent "interviews" with Manny Machado and Klay Thompson.

Cynthia rarely came to the TGIFs and when she did, it was with her boyfriend. However, on one occasion she came with a girlfriend, Kira, and made a point of introducing her to Steve. Clearly, Kira had been well briefed by Cynthia. After having told Steve that she worked in the sales department of a Ford dealership, she told him that she was a Golden State Warriors fan and asked him if he thought they could win another championship. They sat at the bar and talked sports and TV shows.

There was a rather hazy sequence of events as the evening wound down. It ended with Kira inviting herself to his apartment. She used his bathroom and when she came out she started to kiss him. "You don't have to be shy with me, Steve." And suddenly they were on his bed with her on top of him. He was terrified. She started to unzip his jeans and he pushed her away. She thought he was playing, laughed and jumped back on top of him. This time he pushed her so hard that she fell off the bed.

"What are you doing, Steve? Are you a crazy, Steve? Don't you want me, Steve?"

All Steve could do was to roll over on the bed and bury his face in the pillow. Kira sat next to him and stroked his head. "What's the matter, Steve? I'm not going to hurt you, Steve. Did something bad happen to you when you were a kid? My dad used to hurt me when I was a kid. That's why my mom threw him out. My stepdad's not much better, but he knows my mom would kill him if ever he laid a hand on me."

"I'm sorry. I'm sorry. I didn't mean to hurt you."

"I know you didn't, Steve. I'm not angry with you. Cynthia told me that you're a really nice guy and I still believe her. I'm going to leave now. I'd still like to see you again. Call me when you're ready, Steve."

At the office, he may have been the looking-good Steve on the outside, but he felt absolutely miserable. He had made such a fool of himself. There was no way that Kira would want to see him again, let alone kiss him and everything else. He was sure Kira would tell Cynthia about what had happened between them, but Cynthia continued to be her usual friendly self. Maybe Kira hadn't said anything. Maybe that meant that she really did want to see him again. However, Marty, who had an uncanny knack of homing in on Steve's weak spots, was quick to pounce.

"What's with the long face, Steve?" "Did you bet on the wrong team, Steve?" Steve couldn't tell Marty that it was Steve himself who was on the losing team. To say that he had fumbled the ball on the goal line didn't do justice to how he felt.

Steve called Mrs. Felice. He told her that he wanted to thank her again for the Thanksgiving dinner. Given that had been several months ago, he knew that must have sounded pretty lame but he just wanted an excuse to talk to her, to talk to somebody sympathetic. She suggested they meet one day during their lunch break. Their offices were fairly close and it would be easy to meet at a nearby coffee shop that she often went to.

Steve usually ate his lunch in the office kitchen and, whether he liked it or not, Marty would usually join him. So, on the day that Steve was to meet Mrs. Felice, Marty was like a dog worrying at a bone.

"Going out to lunch, are we, Steve?" "Got a lunch date, have we, Steve?" "Who's the unlucky lady, Steve?" As much as Steve would have liked to say, "Fuck you, Marty", he was quite happy with, "You should try getting out yourself one of these days, Marty."

When they met, Mrs. Felice asked him about his job and if he'd thought about going to night school—the local community colleges had lots of courses and diplomas that could lead to more job opportunities for him. She thought he would be eligible for tuition assistance, and she could help him find out about that if he was interested. She then changed the subject. "You're looking good, Steve. I bet you can't keep the girls away. At Thanksgiving, you never really told me about your girlfriend. You do have a girlfriend, don't you Steve?"

"Yes…I mean no. I mean sort of."

"A sort-of girlfriend, Steve? Does she have a sort-of name?"

"Kira…but, but, I don't want to talk about her right now, Mrs. Felice."

"That's quite alright, Steve. And, Steve, don't forget, it's Eva now."

Just at that moment Steve saw Mr. Whitworth come into the coffee shop. He was one of the directors of the firm where Steve worked. Although he was sure Mr. Whitworth didn't know who he was, Steve was surprised when Mr. Whitworth gave a big smile as he walked by. But then Steve realized it was Eva whom Mr. Whitworth had smiled at.

"Eva, I didn't know you knew Mr. Whitworth."

"I've no idea who that is, Steve."

"He's the guy who smiled at you when he walked past our table just now."

"Oh that guy. Never seen him before."

She laughed. "Guys sometimes smile at girls, you know, Steve, even if they don't know them. I'm sure you do it all the time."

Why did Mr. Whitworth smile at Eva? Steve looked at her again. She must be pretty old to have two kids about his age but, come to think of it, she didn't really look that old. She didn't look like a film star or anything, but she had a warm and friendly face, bright brown eyes, and she had big hair. She looked a bit like the school counselor in *Friday Night Lights*. Steve had really liked that show: high school kids making out all the time and playing football, and a counselor to put them straight whenever they got into trouble. For Steve, who'd spent most of his adolescence trying to make himself invisible in various foster homes, it looked like an idyllic existence.

"Time to go, Steve. If you're not going out on a date with your sort-of girlfriend this Friday, why don't you come over?

Tina and her baby are coming, and Gary's coming too. He's a sports fan like you. We're going to have pizza and watch some basketball. Some family time will do you good."

Steve couldn't wait till Friday came around. He didn't get invited to peoples' homes and wasn't sure what was expected, but you surely couldn't go wrong by showing up with a six-pack of Michelob. But when he arrived he found Eva by herself.

"The baby's sick, so Tina and Gary won't be coming over. But don't worry, I've still ordered pizza. And you've brought some beer. We'll have a nice evening."

Steve was in his element: drinking beer, eating pizza and explaining to his apparently appreciative audience of one about pick-and-roll plays, faulting the losing coach for misusing his time-outs, and other tactical mistakes at critical points in the game.

After the game they went into the kitchen to make some coffee. "Well, Steve, I hope you didn't mind spending the evening with an old lady when you could've been out partying with your sort-of girlfriend, Kira."

"You're not old, Eva. And Kira isn't really my girlfriend. She wanted to be my girlfriend but…"

"But what?"

"I…I panicked."

"Panicked how?"

"I…I don't want to talk about it."

"I understand, Steve. I really do. You had a rotten childhood. I've seen enough to know. It makes it difficult to trust anyone, doesn't it?"

"Yes."

"But you trust me, don't you, Steve?"

"Yes."

Eva stroked his cheek and took his hand. "Come with me, Steve," and she led him to her bedroom. He didn't feel at all afraid. He let her undress him and do all sorts of wonderful things to him. When he came he collapsed on top of her and burst into tears. She held him for a long time.

For the next few weeks, Steve went over to Eva's whenever they knew she would be by herself. She always offered him a snack or something to drink, but he would just throw himself at her, drag her to her bedroom, and tear off her clothes. She would tell him not to be so impatient, to slow down, to make love to her slowly. After one intense session of lovemaking she asked him if he'd had any contact with Kira.

"Of course not. She's not my girlfriend. You are."

"I'm not your girlfriend, Steve. I'm your friend, a very intimate one, but not your girlfriend. I'm too old to be your girlfriend."

"I don't understand. I love you."

"You don't love me, Steve. Don't confuse making love to me with being in love with me. You need a girl your own age. Someone you can go out with, have fun with. Someone you can introduce to your friends. I don't think you realize what a wonderful young man you are, and I've loved every minute we've spent together. But I think it's time we called it a day. Believe me, it's for the best, for both of us. Trust me."

When Steve had first started seeing Eva, his mood at work was very upbeat, practically hyper. Marty quickly homed in. "Score big on your lunch date, did you, Steve?" "What's her name, Steve?" "Better wipe that big grin off your face, Steve, before it splits in half." Steve infuriated Marty by ignoring his taunts when he really wanted to punch him in the face. After Eva told Steve that she could no longer see him, Marty immediately picked up on Steve's despondent mood. "Got that long face again, Steve?" "Trouble in paradise, Steve?" "Been dumped for another guy, Steve?" All Steve could do was to curse Marty in his mind, and beat him to pulp in his dreams. He also dreamed about Eva and struggled to understand why she had pushed him away.

A few weeks later Steve was on an office errand that took him past the coffee shop where he and Eva had met. He looked in the window and saw Eva sitting at a table. She was smiling and laughing. There was a man standing by her table. It was Mr. Whitworth. When Steve got back to the office he immediately went to Cynthia's desk and asked her for Kira's phone number.

They met at the same bar where they'd first met. They had a beer and made awkward small talk. Then they went to his apartment. She used his bathroom and when she came out Steve started kissing her.

"So what's different now, Steve?"

He told her how sorry, terribly sorry, he was about last time. The way she had been so nice to him about it made him realize how much he liked her, but it had taken him a long time to summon up the confidence to call her. He led her to his bedroom and undressed her. He made love to her slowly. The looking-good Steve was now the self-confident Steve.

Kira realized all of Steve's sexual fantasies. It seemed as though there was no limit to the ways they could please each other. She would talk dirty to him. "Fuck me, Steve," and a whole lot more. The last time anyone had said "Fuck" to Steve, and meant it, was the neighborhood drunk who would sometimes show up outside his apartment building; but then it was "Fuck you, man" when Steve wouldn't give him any money. But now it was a girl, his girl, saying deliciously dirty things to him. Steve took Kira to his office's TGIF and introduced her to his coworkers as his girlfriend.

It was difficult to believe that in a few short months he had progressed from the nobody Steve, to the looking-good Steve, to Steve the super-stud. For that is how he felt now, and how he sensed his coworkers saw him. Cynthia would still give him a nice smile, but now her smile seemed flirtatious and there was, perhaps, the hint of a gleam in her eye. Marty now seemed almost deferential. There had been an office re-organization and Steve and Marty were now called Office Specialists, although their duties seemed to be the same as before when they had been called Office Assistants. However, now it was Marty who went to the deli to collect the sandwiches and it really was, "Do you want anything from the deli, Steve?" And his coworkers asked for his opinion. Marty asked him what he thought about the new girl who worked in the records department, and his sports-talk coworkers asked for his advice on what bets to place on various games. He had definitely achieved elevated status. He was now alpha-Steve.

One day Marty was out sick and Steve went to the deli to collect the sandwiches. He hadn't been there for quite some time.

"Long time no see, Steve," "You're looking good, Steve," and "I hear you've got yourself a girl, Steve." Frank wanted to talk about a recent college game. He had a beef about one of the coaches and wanted Steve's opinion. Usually, by this time of the season, Steve would have "interviewed" most of the top coaches and would have had plenty to say to Frank. But his evenings and weekends were so taken up with Kira that he was no longer up to speed on college basketball and had to bluff his way through the conversation. Steve felt he had let Frank down. That night he stayed up late studying the statistics and online discussions of the teams involved in the game Frank had wanted to talk about. He made a point of going back to the deli the next day and giving Frank a detailed analysis of the game in question.

Steve and Kira were now spending most of their weekends together. She often slept over at his apartment on Saturday nights, and kept a few clothes and toiletries there. They spent most of their time in bed or watching TV. They rarely went out, and when they did it was just to pick up something to eat, or to go to the liquor store. One weekend Kira came over with a pile of movies and said that they should spend more time talking to each other, and that she wanted to watch some of her favorites old movies with him. These included *When Harry Met Sally, You've Got Mail, Pretty Woman,* and *Dirty Dancing.* Steve liked lying on the sofa with Kira snuggled up next to him, and between movies they had sex. Kira did most of the talking: what she liked about the movies they'd been watching, little incidents at work, the fights she was having with her stepdad, and the arguments he and her mom would have about her staying at Steve's. She told Steve that she and her mom were really close and that's why she was still living at home. But it wasn't a lot of fun. Her stepdad was always picking on her and she didn't like the way he looked at her. She felt it was time to move out, to find a place of her own or a roommate. Sometimes she would tell Steve how happy he made her feel.

And then, one Sunday, Kira dropped a bombshell. She told him that she loved him. She wanted him to know that it wasn't just about the sex. She wanted to know if he loved her. It was the first time anybody had told Steve that they loved him. Everywhere he went people were saying it to each other. Just about every phone call he overheard in the supermarket ended with "Love you," and NFL championship games ended with huge sweaty men hugging each other and saying, "I love you, man." Even when he was the nobody Steve, he believed that one day someone would say, "I love you, Steve," albeit in some vague, distant future. Eva had never told Steve that she loved him, and when he said, "I love you" to her she had told him, in effect, that he didn't know what he was talking about. It was all very confusing.

But maybe with Kira it would be different. Over the past few months, everything he could have possibly wanted— short of actually talking to Michael Jordan at a bar—was his. He was the somebody Steve, the alpha-status Steve, the Steve with the hot girl who would say, "Fuck me, Steve", and who was now saying "I love you, Steve." And now she was asking, "Do you love me, Steve?" He wondered if Kira had been making him watch all those sappy romantic movies to get him in the mood to say sappy romantic things to her. He knew she wanted to hear him say "I love you too, Kira," and that would have made her wildly happy. But he wasn't sure if that was how he felt, and even if it was, he had conditioned himself to avoid being hurt. After all, maybe Kira didn't really mean it when she said, "I love you, Steve." It was so difficult to know if he could trust her, or trust himself. He just didn't know what to do or what to say, so he said nothing. He wished he could ask Eva for her advice.

On Mondays he always got up early to trim his beard—an intricate operation that required the use of a special attachment on his electric razor. But on this particular Monday, the day after Kira had asked him if he loved her, he decided it was too much bother and gave himself a clean shave. Nobody at work seemed to notice except Marty, of course. "What's with the new look, Steve?" "Looking smooth, Steve." "Time for a change, Marty." By the end of the week Marty had shaved off his beard, too. When Steve saw Kira that weekend she stroked his face and told him that she liked him clean-shaven. Although the beard made him look sexy, it scratched her face. She told him that it was his turn to choose the movies, and she snuggled up to him on the sofa as they watched classic sports movies like *Rudy*, *The Natural*, *Bull Durham*, and *Rocky*. She didn't do much talking and didn't stay the night. She told him that she had to spend that Sunday helping her mother with something.

Over the next few weeks there was no more talk of love. For Steve that was a relief, but there was a side of him that wanted to hear Kira say, "I love you, Steve" again. The magic words that everybody else was bandying around all the time had only been said to him once before, and that was by Kira. If she were to say it to him again he would now say something. He had thought about that a lot. Maybe he could say that he liked her, *really* liked her (that was true). Or meeting her was the best thing that had ever happened to him (that was true). Or that every time they had sex he felt really close to her (that was true, too). There were lots of nice things he could say that he knew she would like, but they always fell short of him saying that one word he knew she wanted to hear. But he just couldn't say it. Not just yet.

The office manager—the one who had rebranded Steve and Marty as "Office Specialists"—decided to introduce a dress code. She said that as a premier accounting firm it was important that everyone looked professional even if they didn't meet with clients—so no more jeans in the office. For Steve, that was not a problem. He replaced his black jeans with the black pants he had worn when he was making the transition to his looking-good outfit. But soon there were real problems with his office wardrobe. First, he lost his glasses. Of course, Marty was immediately on his case. "Where're your glasses, Steve?" "Can I help you cross the hallway, Steve?" "Ever heard of contacts, Marty?" However, nobody else at work seemed to notice that he wasn't wearing glasses anymore. That was also the case with Kira. Although she had seen them when they first met, he didn't wear them when they were together. But then real disasters struck. He somehow got copier ink on his sport coat. The cleaner said regular dry-cleaning wouldn't remove the stain and it would have to be sent away to a cleaning specialist. It would take a week. Steve was sure that his supervisor would give him a hard time if he came to work wearing a crew neck without his sport coat. But it wasn't worth buying a new one—after all he'd only be without it for a few days—so he got out his old beige shirt and red tie. But, of course, he had to put up with Marty. "Somebody steal your jacket, Steve?" "What's with the shirt and tie, Steve?" "Going for an interview, are you, Steve?" "Anything to get away from you, Marty." But worse was yet to come. A couple of days later, when coming home from work, Steve tripped over the neighborhood drunk who had passed out at the bottom of the stairs to his apartment. The fall tore his black pants. As soon as he saw the tear he knew that he would have to go to work in his old brown pants till the end of the week when he could go shopping for a new pair of black pants. Now it was Steve's turn to say, "Fuck you, man." He was really angry.

So there he was back in his old brown pants, beige shirt and red tie, no glasses and clean-shaven; just as he had been when he was the nobody Steve, the before-Eva Steve, the before-Kira Steve. He knew it was only for a few days, but he felt strangely naked in his old outfit. It hurt, but what hurt even more was when the office manager said, "Glad to see you're dressing sensibly, Steve." Marty didn't help matters either. "Back in the old brown pants are we, Steve?" "Is brown the new black, Steve?" For once, Steve didn't have a put-down and found himself telling Marty how he had torn his black pants.

"Never mind, Steve. I guess Kira never sees you in pants anyway."

"Fuck you, Marty."

*   *   *

At first I thought Steve was joking when he said, "Fuck you, Marty." But he really meant it. He was really mad at me. I thought he was going to hit me. I guess he didn't like my joke about him and his girl. I've always liked Steve. He's a bit like a big brother to me. Of course, I wouldn't want him to know that, so that's why I always give him a hard time. He's cool. I liked the way he started coming to work with a close-cut beard like those guys in the sports car commercials. That gave me the idea of growing a beard too. But I grew mine longer. Wouldn't want him to think I was a copycat. He knows everything about sports: football, basketball, hockey, everything. Man, he's a sports pro. He could be on ESPN. And then there's his girlfriend, Kira. She's hot. I guess the hot girls like the quiet types like Steve. I'm a noisy kind of guy. I guess that's why I don't have a girl. Maybe I shouldn't have teased Steve about his pants and Kira. He's still not talking to me.

*   *   *

Kira's like a little sister to me. I'm glad I introduced her to Steve. She tells me that he's the real deal. She's started staying over at his place on the weekends. "And..." I ask, and she just gives me a huge grin. Says it all. Makes me look at Steve in a new light. He always seemed like a nice guy—quiet and polite, so different from that loudmouth

Marty. I wasn't sure why Steve started coming to work with a close trimmed beard and glasses, and a sport coat over a crewneck. But it looked pretty cool and he seemed so happy when I told him that he was looking good. I have the feeling that nobody had ever told him that before. He seems very tense right now. Apparently Marty said something that upset him. Something to do with the old brown pants he's started wearing again. I don't care what he wears. The main thing is that he makes Kira happy. At the moment there seems to be a bit of a problem between them. She's worried that he doesn't love her as much as she loves him. I hope they sort it out.

* * *

It's a pity that Steve hardly comes to my deli anymore. I like him. I always enjoy talking sports with him. He really knows his stuff. Not like that loudmouth Marty who picks up the sandwiches now. Still, he entertains me with office gossip. He tells me that Steve's girl, Kira, is really hot. He's sure she's hot because Steve comes to work on Monday mornings with a big grin on his face. And now Marty is going on about how Steve is mad at him about something. Something to do with Kira. Something to do with Steve's brown pants. I've no idea what it's all about. I think what Marty needs is a girl of his own.

* * *

I'm glad Cynthia introduced me to Steve. I felt so badly for him when he couldn't do it the first time, and I didn't think he'd want to see me again. And when he did, he was completely different. I don't know what happened to make him change so much, but no complaints. He's such a sweet guy. I feel safe with him...and it's the best sex, ever. At the moment Steve seems really upset about something that loudmouth Marty said to him. Steve won't tell me what it's about. Makes me think it was something rude about me, and Steve doesn't want to tell me because he thinks it would upset me. I'm sure that means he loves me. I just want him to say it to me. I think it would make him feel a lot better. I think we should move in together.

* * *

I probably know more about Steve than anybody else. I was his caseworker at Social Services when he was in his teens. The system let him down badly on more than one occasion. When he was twelve he was put in a foster home that hadn't been properly vetted. The husband had a record of domestic violence—something that Steve's caseworker at the time claimed not to have known. But despite everything, Steve still managed to be a really good-natured kid and never got into trouble. I had him over for Thanksgiving a few times and he would sit there quietly while my two girls teased him and my ex-husband scowled at him. Running into a former coworker at Social

Services a while ago made me think about Steve again. I had this sudden impulse to contact him and have him over for Thanksgiving. He was still that same good-natured kid I remembered, still lacking in self-confidence except when he talked about sports. But now he's more than a kid. He's grown into a good-looking young man. When we met that time for coffee he had a new look: a neatly trimmed three-day beard and a jacket over a dark crewneck. He looked very cute. I was surprised when he told me that he didn't have a girlfriend, only a sort-of girlfriend called Kira. It's not difficult to guess what he meant when he told me he'd panicked when she made a move on him. I hope he tried to get together with her after I told him I couldn't see him anymore. Was it wrong of me to have seduced him? If it gave him the self-confidence to be with a girl of his own age, I'm not going to feel too guilty about it. And I enjoyed being with him. By the way, a funny thing happened recently. I was in the coffee shop where I often go on my lunch break when a middle-aged guy tried a new pick-up line on me. He came up to my table and said, "I saw you here a few weeks ago with a young man who works for my company. I hope he wasn't bothering you." It was difficult not to laugh.

* * *

I think everybody at the office knows I got mad at Marty and told him to fuck off. It wasn't the first time he'd asked for it, and it felt really good to finally let him have it. I didn't like Marty suggesting that Kira was some sort of nympho. Marty can be such a jerk. Most of the time he's OK and can be quite funny, but his big mouth is just too much sometimes. The trouble is that what he said made me realize that Kira is really special to me. Eva's also special to me. At first I was really mad at her for dumping me, but now I'm with Kira I understand why she ended it. I know this sounds weird, but I'd like to introduce Kira to Eva. Maybe we could all be friends. I think I'm going to ask Kira to move in with me.

BLUE GUITAR

For a few precious moments I was alone in the gallery facing Picasso's iconic masterpiece. The angular lines and flat blue planes of the old guitarist spoke to me as they have spoken to countless others:

> *They said, "You have a blue guitar,*
> *You do not play things as they are."*
> *He replied, "Things as they are,*
> *Are changed upon the blue guitar."*

His head was horizontal, his eyes almost blind, staring intently at the ground. Yet could there be the faintest hint of a smile on his face? Was he playing his last mournful song or was he strumming a joyful distillation of all life's experiences—his interpretation of all he had seen and all those he had met on his timeless journey.

> *They said, "You have a blue guitar,*
> *You do not see people as they are."*
> *He replied, "People as they are,*

Are different when played on my guitar."

Was he blue because he was near death or because he had just materialized out of the sky? Was he a blue deity haunting the white walls of a blank imagination, challenging the minds of those who came to see him? Or was he about to fade away into the empyrean and become a spirit who would induce me to look into the darkest corners of my imagination? Were his long, blue, and almost translucent fingers that plucked the guitar strings the hands of death, or the timeless instruments of Apollo bringing music to Daphne? Was he so hunched and angular because he was so tired and old, and doubled over with the pain of infinite age? Or was he trying to economize his place in time and space so that he could see more and be noticed less? Was he sitting cross-legged and ragged on the ground because he was so poor and destitute, or because he was so rich and at ease in the experience of life and beyond earthly needs?

I began to say, "I do not know your blue guitar..." when a little girl, perhaps four or five years old with curly brown hair, skipped out of nowhere in front of the picture and, with her back to me, stopped and stared at the masterpiece. Hands on her hips, a tilt to her head, and a fidget in her feet. Suddenly she chortled and bounced away. Maybe she could see and understand it all. Maybe she could play the blue guitar. Her fleeting presence broke my dream and I had to leave the world of imagination and return to the rational light.

I was feeling very pleased with my thoughts about Picasso's painting, and the appearance of the little girl would add a delightful note to the article I was writing about the gallery. But then I heard a voice call out, "Hey you." There was nobody in the gallery, yet the voice was definitely cast in my direction. "Yes, you. I'm talking to you."

The voice, old and gruff, seemed to be coming from the direction of the picture. "Yes you, asshole. Just because I'm almost blind doesn't mean I can't see you. You seem to be the one who's blind. You're looking right at me."

Talking to pictures in a public gallery risks ridicule, but the gallery appeared to be empty. I whispered, "Are you talking to me?"

"Who the hell do you think I'm talking to, dick-head? And why are you whispering? You're the only one here right now. Standing there thinking all that drivel about me and the blue guitar."

This was insane. "How did you, whoever you are, know what I was thinking?"

"Of course you know who I am. I'm *The Old Guitarist*. Who else could I be?"

"But how did you know what I was thinking?"

"All that talk about art being the lie that reveals the truth is the wrong way around. It's the painting itself that reveals the truth about the artist and the viewer. And as for you, my friend, any self-respecting painting can see that you're just another snotty art critic…"

"Now look here…"

"Now, now…don't get touchy. I'm doing you a big favor by talking to you. If you get off your high horse, I'll tell you whom I really am. You want to know, don't you?"

"Well, yes. I do."

"OK, then. Jump in. I could do with some more company."

The 'more company' sounded ominous. Would this picture turn out to be some sort of Bluebeard's Castle for art critics? But I was really curious. I had studied every scholarly work about this painting and the artist, but maybe there was some hidden secret that the old man would reveal, a secret that could make me famous. However, I didn't understand how I was meant to 'jump in'. At that moment, I could have sworn the old man winked at me and suddenly I found myself in the picture crouched on the ground next to him.

"So what was it you wanted to ask me?"

"Well, a lot of things. But first, what should I call you? And second, how come you speak such good English? I thought you were meant to be an illiterate beggar from the streets of Barcelona."

"You can call me Luis. And as for speaking English, I've been stuck in this gallery since 1926 and have had to listen to an endless parade of academics and curators pontificating about me. What a bunch of windbags. All those long fancy words that say so little. But it's been a good way to learn English. And then there're all the janitors and security guards working here. What a foul-mouthed bunch they are, but they've certainly broadened my vocabulary. There was one guard in particular who worked on the night shift. He would stand in front of me and say 'How ya doin', old man' and then call me every obscenity under the sun. Reminded me of Pablo. And as for being an illiterate beggar, I hear that I'm currently worth at least $150M. So how much are you worth, my friend? Compared to me, you're the beggar. Anyhow, you're taking up far too much space in front of me. There's much more room behind me. Go round the back and sit with Germaine."

Now this made sense: recent X-ray analyses had revealed the partial figure of a woman behind the old man. Some art historians have suggested it might have been Germaine Pichot. Suddenly I found myself behind Luis sitting next to a naked woman with large breasts.

"*Bonjour monsieur*, have you come to visit little Odette?"

"I thought you were Germaine. Luis said you were Germaine."

"*Non*, I am Odette, Germaine's friend."

Being a knowledgeable art critic has its advantages. "So you must be Louise Lenoir."

"You know me, *monsieur*? I don't recall having slept with you."

"You're quite famous, you know."

She looked very pleased with the compliment and stuck her breasts in my face. "Do you find me attractive, *chéri*? Would you like to have me? It's been such a long time since I've had a man. Just a quickie. Just like Pablo. I could make you famous, *chéri*. You could say that you have slept with one of Pablo's models."

So what's new, I thought.

"Don't worry about Luis, he can't see us. He likes to listen, though. That's all he could do in Pablo's studio, stuck up on the easel all the time. When Pablo wasn't painting him, he was screwing me or Germaine, or anyone else he could find. *Quel cochon*! Ah, Pablo...he thought he was a big bull, but he was just a little pig."

I'd never been propositioned by a model in a picture before and wasn't sure how to respond, but I needed to act quickly. Odette was squirming around like a cat in heat and just about to pounce when we heard voices. Even if we couldn't be seen we might be heard. I motioned to Odette to stop so I could listen to what was being said. One of the voices sounded familiar. I peered over Luis's shoulder and could see one of the art history professors I knew from the University of Chicago. He was with a young woman, probably a graduate student he was trying to impress. His words sounded all too familiar.

"Notice the angular lines and flat blue planes of the old guitarist as they speak to us as they have spoken to countless others. This timeless picture immediately brings to mind Wallace Stevens' immortal lines:

> *They said, 'You have a blue guitar,*
> *You do not play things as they are.'*
> *He replied, 'Things as they are,*

Are changed upon the blue guitar.'

You know, Michelle, standing here…with you…in front of this great work, only serves to remind me, remind us, about the transience of human existence…"

Luis was trying to not burst out laughing. "Listen to that pompous ass-hole, my friend. Just like you. He's spouting the same nonsense you were thinking just a few minutes ago. Trying to impress the girl. You guys are all the same. And this obsession with the blue guitar, it's all absolute nonsense."

I didn't like having my scholarship challenged so bluntly. "How so, may I ask?"

"Use your eyes, Dumbo. The guitar is brown. It's not f***ing blue, it's f***ing brown. I should know. I've been playing it for well over a hundred years. If you arty types would just use your eyes instead of your big mouths, the world would be a much better place. Anyhow, it seems that the coast is clear now. Nobody will see you leave. Nice talking to you, my friend."

And suddenly there I was, standing in front of *The Old Guitarist* again. It was difficult to make sense of it all, yet I could definitely catch a whiff of cheap cologne on my coat, along with a couple of short black hairs that must have come from Odette. Whatever had happened, and how it had happened, was difficult to make sense of, but it had happened. The cologne and hairs were proof. I also realized that I'd made an important discovery: the figure behind *The Old Guitarist* was Louise "Odette" Lenoir. And I could prove it by getting DNA matches with the hairs I had just picked up. But how could I explain how I had acquired them from the painting? Hmm...that could be tricky. But before I did anything else I really needed a cup of strong black coffee to clear my head. I thought I would walk down to the second level and see if the Balcony Café was still open.

Suddenly, the little girl I'd seen earlier appeared a few feet in front of me and waved to me to follow her. Strange... but then the day was already so strange I felt compelled to follow. She skipped down the stairs—it was difficult to keep up—and before I knew it I was in Gallery 262 staring at Hopper's *Nighthawks*. I thought I heard the little girl giggle, but when I looked around she had disappeared.

Ah, *Nighthawks*. What a painting...its cool, remote tones were suddenly very soothing after my recent adventure with Luis and Odette. A few minutes meditation in front of it was just what I needed. I was just starting to feel relaxed when I noticed the counterman in the picture waving to me through the diner window. He seemed to be miming that he could pour me a cup of coffee and gestured for me to come in. I gave him a questioning shrug since I couldn't see an entrance in the painting. He pointed to his left indicating that the diner entrance was around the side of the picture, and suddenly I was inside. The man sitting by himself with his back to the window said, without looking at me, "You can sit on the stool next to me. You're not in the composition so no one will notice you."

This was absolutely thrilling: the man was reputed to be Hopper himself. He held up his hand like a policemen stopping traffic. "Yes, I am…and please no gushing about how much you love my paintings, everyone does."

I explained to him that I was the art critic for The Washington Post, and was working on an article about the Art Institute of Chicago. Would he mind if I asked him a few questions?

"I suppose you want to ask me the usual questions about the aesthetics of isolation, the soliloquies of separation, the miasmal mists of loneliness, the dysphoria of darkness, the haunting tones of hopelessness, blah, blah, blah, blah…all absolute hogwash."

"No, no, no," I protested, "your art is the very essence of…"

"The very essence of what?"

I had the feeling I was about to be crushed. "I mean…I mean, you're the greatest American painter of the twentieth century."

He gave a little snort. "OK, mister art critic, look at that couple at the end of the counter, the guy with the hawk-like nose and the redheaded dame. What do you see?"

That famous couple has been the subject of endless speculation, scholarship, poetry and fiction. Although it was generally accepted that the artist had used his wife as the model for the woman, the identity of the man was unknown.

I realized that I now had another prize in my grasp. All I had to do was get Hopper to tell me who hawk-nose was. But first I had to answer his question. Impress him. Gain his confidence. "Well, what we see is a profound study of emotional interiority, the seen and the unseen of quiet desperation, the known and the unknown of loneliness, the concealed calculus of failing human connectivity..."

Hopper and the counterman burst out laughing. "Just as you said when you saw him looking in the window, Mr. Hopper. This guy's a real bozo."

Along with being called an asshole, a dick-head, and a Dumbo, I was now being called a bozo. I could imagine claiming that I'd been called a bozo by Edward Hopper might gain me some kudos at literary cocktail parties but then, as with Odette's hairs, it would be rather difficult to explain how that had come about. But being called a bozo by a mere counterman was too much. No tip for you, bozo! But I held my tongue.

"Don't mind him," said Hopper gesturing towards the counterman, "Gary here is quite the live-wire. Aren't you, Gary?"

"Yes sir, Mr. Hopper. I sure am."

"Let me explain to you what Gary and me were laughing about. Everyone has got this whole thing wrong. Sure, I enjoy evoking lonely nighttime scenes, that's what I do better than anyone else, but it was all staged. It was part of a little game that Jo, my wife, and I like to play. What we do is this. Jo..." and he pointed to the redhead, "sits by herself at the end of the counter looking lonely and we wait for a guy to come in and try his luck with her. We have one here right now. He's offered her a cigarette and is telling her some sob story about how his wife has just left him and how he's just lost his job. You know, the usual lines that losers use in late-night, diner scenes in 1940's movies. I just sit and watch and take notes. It's a great source of ideas for my paintings. And, of course, I'm here in case there's any trouble. And Gary's in on the game, too. Packs a 45, don't you Gary?" Gary grinned and patted a bulge under his white counterman's jacket. And don't worry, hawk-nose can't hear what I'm saying, he's frozen in time."

"So you mean…"

"That's right, my friend, I haven't a clue who he is. And there you were thinking I'd tell you his name and how you'd be able to score a great coup in the art world with your discovery. And, anyhow, if I told you, how would you be able to explain how Hopper had told you who he was?"

At that point Gary, who I was hoping would bring me a cup of coffee, lent over the counter and sniffed my coat. "Mr. Hopper, sir, this bozo's wearing perfume. I thought there was something wrong with him. We really don't want his sort in the diner. Bad for business."

"You're right, Gary. Time for you go, my friend."

And suddenly there I was, standing in front of *Nighthawks* again. I was miffed by my abrupt dismissal from the diner. It wasn't my fault that Odette had left traces of her perfume on me. I also needed that cup of coffee, the one that Gary never gave me. What a bozo. And then, out of the blue, there was that little girl again gesturing for me to follow her. What could I do but obey? She raced through the next gallery, but it was impossible not to stop for a moment and look at Grant Wood's *American Gothic*. Of course some people say it's one of the great works of 20th century American art but I beg to differ. I won't say "in my humble opinion", because I'm not a humble person. Art critics are not humble people. While the painting may have some charm as an example of regional art, it's been totally debased into a plaything of popular culture—even to the point of being sculptured in butter. That's Iowa for you! And then there're the countless morons who pose and preen in front of it, even sticking their faces through cutouts of the two characters: the sour-faced old farmer and his equally sour-faced wife—or is it his daughter? Ha! In those backward rural communities, who knows what went on?

Out of the corner of my eye, I could see the little girl impatiently beckoning me to hurry up and follow her. It was difficult to resist giving the picture a derisive sneer of disapproval before leaving the gallery, but as I turned to leave I felt myself being grabbed by the neck and thrown on the ground. When I looked up I found myself staring at the beady, wire-framed, eyes of the old farmer and the prongs of his pitchfork inches away from my face. To say he looked sour would be an understatement. He was talking to the woman. "See, Nan, what did I tell you? One of them out-of-towners, a city slicker, come to sneer at us hard-working farming folks. I can spot 'em a mile off. Anybody who doesn't like butter can't be trusted. And you saw the way he looked at you. We all know what he was thinking. And he smells of perfume, too. A real pervert."

"Even worse, Byron, he could be one of them sissy art critics. Gives me the creeps. What shall we do with him? Feed him to the hogs?"

They both laughed. I didn't know what was worse: being called a snotty art critic by Luis, or a sissy art critic by this...this sour-faced farm girl called Nan. But before I could protest, they picked me up by the shoulders and dragged me into their Gothic house and threw me into a dark room—probably a torture chamber where they dismembered their victims into pig food. The woman opened a pair of window shutters and I saw that I was in a dentist's office. I was pushed into the dentist's chair and the man was shining a light in my face.

"Us Iowans are real friendly folks, you know, but we don't like strangers coming into town making fun of us." He picked up his drill and motioned to the woman to start it up with a foot-pedal. I wanted to tell them that I didn't want to end up as hog fodder in a Norman Bates movie; but what was the point, they wouldn't know who he was.

"Now tell us mister city-slicker, why are you really here? What's your game? And what's your problem with butter?"

I didn't know what to say. I had no idea how I could explain to them that I was the art critic for The Washington

Post writing an article about the Art Institute of Chicago, an article that was deliberately not going to mention their painting.

"Lost your tongue have you? Well, open wide and I'll give you a free filling."

At that point I passed out. When I came to I found myself lying on a grassy bank by a river. Sunlight was playing on the water giving it an almost confetti like brilliance. As I looked around I could see groups of people sitting or standing, casting long shadows. Women with parasols, men in top hats, children and dogs, and even a monkey on a leash. I could hear the murmur of voices speaking in French. I had died and gone to pointillist heaven! I was at La Grande Jatte! Lying on the ground nearby, smoking a pipe, was a big handsome fellow with bare muscular arms. And a little further away was a woman standing by the water's edge with a fishing pole. I wondered what she was hoping to catch. I thought I would try to engage the man in conversation. I didn't think there was any point in telling him that I was the art critic for The Washington Post. I'd pretend I was a tourist who'd got lost. Knowing how much the French hate to speak English, I would try to engage him in French.

"Excusez-moi, monsieur, je suis un touriste. Pouvez-vous me dire où je suis."

He looked at me suspiciously. "Un touriste? Un américain?"

"Oui, je suis américain."

He looked at my head and laughed. "Quel drôle de chapeau!"

To be honest, I couldn't remember which hat I had put on to go to the gallery, and when I took it off I saw it was a fedora, rather like the one Hopper had been wearing in the diner. It looked as though we had a conversational opening.

"C'est un fedora. Voulez-vous l'essayer? Mon nom est Bartholomew. Mes amis m'appellent Bart."

I could see his nose wrinkle in disgust—he must have caught a whiff of Odette's wretched perfume. He waved a clenched fist in my face. "Je ne suis pas votre ami, monsieur. Faites chier!"

After my rough treatment at the hands of those farmer/ dentists in Iowa, I didn't want to get beaten up by some beefy Frenchman, so I walked away quickly. However, it wasn't every day that I could be in Seurat's great masterpiece, so I thought I'd try my luck with the woman with the fishing pole. "Excusez-moi, madame, je suis un touriste. Pouvez-vous me dire où je suis."

She looked at me with a smile. "Un touriste? Un américain?"

"Oui, je suis américain."

She sniffed delicately. "Quel parfum portez-vous?"

"Je ne suis pas sûr. C'est à ma femme."

"Bien sûr, votre femme. Et qu'est-ce que vous me voulez, monsieur?"

"Je voudrais savoir pourquoi vous pêchez?"

"Je pêche pour tout ce que je peux attraper."

Fishing for whatever she could catch—this was getting interesting. I was just about to introduce myself when I saw the Frenchman who had just told me to piss off, now accompanied by a group of men who'd just got out of a rowing boat, run towards me. They all looked very big and strong, and very aggressive. It was clear I was going to be beaten up, very badly beaten up. I could just see the headlines: 'Famous art critic beaten to death in popular Parisian park'. That would be very embarrassing. But how could I escape? At that point somebody grabbed my hand and pulled me out of the painting. It was the little girl. She looked cross. "Where have you been? I've been looking for you *everywhere*. No more going off by yourself. *Promise*? Follow me." And she led me to the next gallery.

I now found myself standing in front of Van Gogh's *Bedroom in Arles*. What a welcome sight! Those cheerful colors, that angular perspective beckoning me in, and that warm inviting bed. Just looking at it was as good as taking a much-needed nap, especially after all my earlier adventures. But then I saw a hand come out from under the bed covers and wave to me. 'Come on in' it seemed to be saying, and sure enough, before I knew it, I found myself in the bed. And next to me was a voluptuous naked woman.

"Who are you?" she said. "I've been waiting up all night for Vincent to come home. He's spending all his time at Café Terrace and comes home stinking of alcohol and cheap whores. But I think you'll do for tonight, *monsieur,* even if your clothes look a bit strange and you smell of cheap Parisian cologne. What's your name?"

"I'm Bartholomew. My friends call me Bart. But who are you?"

"I am Louise Lenoir. My friends call me Odette."

It was clear that I was being taken for a fool, being made the victim of an elaborate hoax. It was time for me to draw a line in the sand. "I don't know what your game is, young lady, but I know for a fact that you cannot be Odette. It's absolutely impossible and, I have to say, I don't like being made a fool of."

"Why is it impossible, *Monsieur Bart*?"

"For a start, Van Gogh painted this bed in 1888. You would have been, at most, a little girl at the time. And..." looking at her ample breasts, "you are most certainly not a little girl. Second, you cannot be in two places at once. I know that you're in the painting with Luis, *The Old Guitarist*. I know that for a fact because I met Odette, the real Odette, there a little earlier today."

"I have to say, *Monsieur Bart,* for one who thinks he's a knowledgeable art critic you are remarkably *stupide*. You are forgetting that this is art. In art everything is possible, even the impossible. I can be whoever I want...whomever you want...whenever I want, and wherever I want. After all, Vincent painted three of these beds. There's one here in Chicago, another in Amsterdam, and another in Paris. Why, later tonight, I could be in Paris if I felt like it, and with another man if I wanted. Perhaps one smarter than you and who didn't smell of cheap cologne."

It was just one insult after another. Now I was being called *stupide* on a day that I had already been called an asshole, a dick-head, a Dumbo, a bozo, and a pervert. Being called a bozo in a Hopper painting was something of a badge of honor, but being called stupid by a woman of dubious morals was just too much. But I again held my tongue. Sorting out her identity could be my chance, maybe my last one of the day, of making an important discovery of art historical importance. "So, *Mademoiselle Odette*, if that is who you truly are, please tell me who Luis's companion really is."

"I'm surprised you haven't worked that out for yourself, *Monsieur Bart*. It was Germaine. We are friends and rivals. Rivals for Pablo. Some nights when he came home so late and so drunk, he couldn't tell the difference between us, and would have who ever he found in his bed. So Germaine often pretended to be me and has kept up this deception since Luis showed up in Pablo's studio and..."

But before Odette could finish her sentence, another voice said, "Are you gossiping about me again, Odette?" And suddenly, in the bed next to Odette and me was Germaine—the woman who had been masquerading as Odette in *The Old Guitarist*. She too was stark naked.

"Ah, *chéri*, I didn't expect to see you again so soon. Perhaps you have changed your mind about my offer?"

Germaine and Odette burst into a fit of giggles and started to whisper to each other. And then Odette, the real Odette, whispered in my ear, "So, *Monsieur Bart,* it's just the three of us in Vincent's bed. We're sure he won't be home tonight so perhaps you would like to play with both of us? *Veux-tu faire un trio avec nous?* That was what Pablo always wanted. *Le cochon.* But we never let him. To think, *Monsieur Bart,* you could do something that he never did. Now that would make you really famous."

And that was an offer I could not refuse.

THE INQUISITION

Andrew opened his laptop and began to type the next scene of his play.

First interview at OGPU headquarters. Moscow, March 4th, 1934.

The office of Lieutenant M. The Lieutenant is sitting behind a desk and studying a folder. A lamp and a small bust of Lenin sit on the desk. A large picture of Stalin hangs on the wall behind the Lieutenant. In front of the desk is an empty chair. There are a series of filing cabinets along one of the walls and a small window in the wall opposite. A guard brings a man into the room and motions him to the desk. The guard stands by the door.

Lieutenant *(friendly tone):* Ah yes, Andrei Ivanovich Suslov. Good afternoon, comrade. Please sit down. We're just making some routine enquiries today. You live in apartment 57 in building 14 on Tyutchev Street?

Suslov: Yes, comrade Lieutenant.

Lieutenant: How well do you know Sergei Mikhailevich Lebedovsky who lives in apartment 43?

Suslov: I hardly know him at all. We exchange greetings when we pass each other on the stairs, but that's about all.

Lieutenant: And your wife, Maria Kirilovna, does she know him?

Suslov: No more than me, comrade Lieutenant.

Lieutenant: But does she know his wife, Ludmila Vasilevna Lebedovskaya?

Suslov: Maybe a little. They gossip sometimes in the communal kitchen. You know how it is, comrade.

Lieutenant: I don't know how it is, comrade. I don't have time to gossip in kitchens. Gossip can be dangerous. Tell me, what is it that women gossip about in kitchens?

Suslov: I'm not sure if I know, either. The price of eggs. Where they can find fabrics to make their dresses. Things like that, I guess.

Lieutenant: Hmm…*(writing in his folder)*…the price of eggs. What were you doing on the evening of February 26th?

Suslov: Let me think…yes, we spent the evening at home listening to a concert on the radio…the Leningrad Philharmonic playing Tchaikovsky's Fourth Symphony.

Lieutenant: So you and Maria Kirilovna spent the whole evening in your apartment?

Suslov: Yes, but around ten o'clock I stepped out for a few minutes.

Lieutenant: Stepped out? And where did you step out to, comrade?

Suslov: Yes. My wife sent me to ask Ludmila Vasilevna if we could borrow some sugar.

Lieutenant: She sent you to the Lebedovskys' apartment to ask for some sugar?

Suslov: Yes, comrade Lieutenant. We had run out of sugar and wanted a few lumps to have with our tea.

Lieutenant: Why had you run out of sugar?

Suslov: Maria Kirilovna wasn't able to find any in the store that day. Shortages, you know.

Lieutenant: Shortages? What shortages? There are no shortages. *(To the guard standing by the door):* Do you know anything about shortages of sugar, soldier?

Soldier: No, comrade Lieutenant.

Lieutenant *(to the guard):* Go and fetch us a bowl of sugar from the canteen. Quick, now.

Total silence in the Lieutenant's office as they wait for the soldier to return. The Lieutenant leafs through the folder on his desk. Suslov fidgets nervously in his chair. The soldier returns with a bowl of sugar lumps.

Lieutenant: See, comrade, there is no shortage of sugar. *(Takes a lump and bites on it.)* Mmm…delicious. Pure Soviet sugar. The best there is. Here, comrade, take a piece. *(Suslov hesitates.)* Really, comrade, take a piece…good. Now where were we? Yes…you went to the Lebedovskys' apartment around ten on the night of February 26th. Just to borrow a few lumps of sugar. Was anyone else there? Maybe the Lebedovskys were having a party?

Suslov: I don't know. I think I heard some people talking and laughing in another room.

Lieutenant: Laughing? What were they laughing about?

Suslov: I don't know, comrade Lieutenant. I didn't stay. I just thanked Ludmila Vasilevna for the sugar and went back to my apartment. That's all I can tell you.

Lieutenant: OK, comrade Suslov, let's recap. On the night of February 26th, at about ten o'clock, you went to the apartment of Sergei Mikhailevich Lebedovsky to ask his wife, Ludmila Vasilevna, for a few lumps of sugar. While you were there you observed that they had a group of visitors who were laughing about something. And then you went back to your apartment.

Suslov: Yes, comrade Lieutenant, that's how it was.

Lieutenant *(closing the file on his desk, his manner is cheerful):* Well, I think that's all for now, comrade. Thank you for your help with our enquiries. You may go now. *(The Lieutenant takes a handful of sugar lumps and quickly twists them up in a sheet of paper.)* And here's some sugar for that pretty little wife of yours. Courtesy Comrade Stalin. We'll call you back if we have any further questions.

Lights dim as Suslov is escorted out of the Lieutenant's office.

* * *

Andrew closed his laptop. He was pleased with how the scene captured the cynical ways OGPU officers toyed with their victims: alternating fake friendliness with veiled threats, confusing them with the importance of trivialities, those lumps of sugar and the price of eggs. It was all a master-class in psychological torture—a set of tricks designed to create uncertainty, plant the seeds of anxiety, and build a climate of fear. The fist in a velvet glove that left the victim certain of the fist in the iron glove to follow. The fist that threatened torture, imprisonment, punishment of their families, the loss of jobs, their apartments, and their dignity. And there was no escape. As Beria once said, "Give us the man, and we'll make the case."

Ideas for the next, more frightening, interview were already forming in Andrew's mind. As always, he had totally immersed himself in the culture and history of the period he was writing about, and for this play he had interviewed children and grandchildren of victims and survivors of Stalin's purges. It was difficult to imagine surviving such a period of insanity and fear. But then, in every era—past, present, and future—insanity is always lurking on the sidelines waiting to storm the field with its team of enablers.

Andrew felt tired. He got up from his desk and stretched. He rubbed the left side of his chest. It felt a bit sore after his morning swim. Maybe a pulled muscle. Something he should probably mention at his annual medical tomorrow. His doctor—a really good guy, almost a friend—would probably insist on an X-ray. Tests and procedures at the clinic always took up too much time, always too much waiting around.

"Ah, Mr. Wallace…Andrew, how are you? It's been a year, hasn't it? Before we start, I just wanted to say how much my wife and I enjoyed your last play. Absolutely brilliant. I hope you're working on another masterpiece."

"I'm fine, Dr. Aaronson. And, yes, I'm working on another play. It's set in the old Soviet Union at the time of the Stalinist purges."

"Fascinating... So, how are you feeling? Have there been any noticeable changes since your last check-up? Shortness of breath, dizziness, headaches, fatigue, strange aches or pains, changes with your bowel movements, urination, libido? You know, the same questions I ask you every year. Anything out of the ordinary?"

"Not really. Perhaps a bit of fatigue, but that's only because I've been going flat out on the new play and a couple of movie scripts."

"And you're exercising regularly? Swimming isn't it?"

"Yes. I still go swimming almost every day. I suppose I should mention that some months ago I felt a bit of a twinge on the left side of my rib cage. It hasn't gone away, but it hasn't stopped me swimming. Some days it hurts a bit more than others, but no big deal. I'm guessing it's just a pulled muscle or a pinched nerve."

"Well, we'll check it all out. Please take off your shirt and lie back on the examination table."

And so the examination proceeded. The chest: short breaths, deep breaths, through the nose, through the mouth, tapping here, tapping there. Clear as a bell. Some careful prodding of the sore area on the rib cage, definitely a painful spot that needed to be X-rayed. The annual humiliation of a prostate exam. Aaronson was a firm believer in the physical exam—the PSA blood test was notorious for false positives.

Andrew wondered what other men thought about, apart from the discomfort, as they went through that uniquely male experience. Andrew thought about his play. False positives, false negatives, positive negatives, negative positives; whatever the permutations of truth and falsehood, the OGPU would always twist things to their advantage. And as for the test itself, there were those grotesque variations with a power hose—a torture that would inflict extreme pain and lasting damage to the victims. A horrible thought, but it was something that could be used in the play.

A nurse took Andrew to another room to draw some blood. The usual tests: cholesterol, blood chemistry, cell counts, and then to Radiology for the chest X-ray. Dr. Aaronson would call in a couple of days to discuss the results.

A call came the next morning from Aaronson's nurse asking Andrew if he could possibly return to the clinic that afternoon. Dr. Aaronson wanted to go over the results of the X-ray in person. Unusual, to be called back so quickly, but Aaronson always went out of his way for Andrew. Maybe it was because Andrew was a famous playwright; but that was unfair, Aaronson was a doctor who cared about all his patients. The X-ray must have revealed something. Couldn't be lung cancer, though. There was absolutely no family history and Andrew had never smoked. Probably a cracked rib, a stress fracture perhaps, something that should get taped up as soon as possible. That must be it, nothing to worry about. By contrast, the OGPU liked to let their victims stew for a few days before calling them back. Being called back to the clinic the next day to review an X-ray was quite different. Aaronson was just being a good doctor taking care of his patient.

"Andrew, thank you so much for coming back at such short notice. I know how busy you are. I wanted to show you the results of your chest X-ray..."

"Let me guess, a cracked rib."

"Well, yes, you do have a cracked rib. You've had it for months. Your daily swims ensured that it never had the chance to heal. You're in such good shape that it didn't slow you down as much as it might have done another person..."

"So, you're going to tape me up and give me some pain medication?"

"I'm afraid that's not the problem, Andrew."

Problem. Comrade, we have a problem. Wasn't that how it usually started? Some small detail: a missing page of a document that didn't exist, an apparent contradiction in your statement about the price of eggs you had made the week before. A problem. The problem. Andrew's problem. And this problem was neither fabricated nor trivial, it was a shocker. The X-ray showed little black gaps on some of the ribs. Bone lesions. The lesions had weakened a rib and caused it to break. Bone lesions, the hallmark of multiple myeloma—a hematological malignancy. Malignancy. The OGPU liked words like that. Before long, Suslov would be a cancer on the State, a societal malignancy. Malignancies had to be stamped out, stamped out ruthlessly, stamped out for the good of the people. And now the malignancy was on Andrew. And now it was real life, not a play.

Just like that, Andrew's world had changed. Really changed. Irreversibly changed. As a playwright, Andrew loved creating shocking moments—those moments that could make an audience gasp. But now it was his own play and he was his own audience for his own shocking moment. He didn't gasp, he couldn't. He could scarcely breathe.

The world seemed to split into two parallel streams of consciousness. In one stream he was listening to Dr. Aaronson who was explaining that as soon as he saw the X-rays he had called his colleague, Dr. Rubin, head of Hematology, and a leading expert in Andrew's condition. Orders for more tests had already been placed: detailed blood work and a complete skeletal survey—top to toe— to determine the extent of the bone damage. All of this needed to be done right away. Dr. Rubin had adjusted his schedule so that he could see Andrew the day after tomorrow to review the test results and discuss the next steps. Dr. Aaronson's tone was calm, his words carefully chosen. It was a conversation he was trained to have. One couldn't pretend it wasn't a very serious situation, he could understand how bleak the outlook must seem, but there'd been huge advances in cancer treatments, and there was still every reason to hope for a good quality of life for several, if not many, years to come.

In the other stream of consciousness, Andrew was listening to himself. But that stream was a turbulent, disorganized cascade of thoughts. The doctors would stamp out his malignancy and maybe he'd be stamped out in the process, just like Suslov was going to be stamped out. And what was he, Andrew, going to tell his ex-wife, Elaine? They had stayed on reasonably friendly terms after their divorce, but how would she react to the news; news he felt compelled to tell her right away. Would she want to help him through it? There was no reason why she should, but then—and this was another shocking realization—who else was there he could count on? And what would he tell the woman he'd been dating recently? And his daughter, Natasha, now at college, how would she react? As far as Andrew could tell, she liked having a famous dad. Famous dads were a source of kudos, famous dads could be useful, but famous dads were the sort of dads who didn't have enough time for their children. As well as they got on now, he could still sense some lingering resentment of his neglect of her when she was growing up. And then there was his work. Would he be able to finish his play? What about the film scripts he was working on? Could he wriggle out of those contracts? And when would he tell Frank, his agent? The guy was really good at his job, but a total drama queen. Andrew didn't want to have to deal with the inevitable Oscar-winning performance that would follow the news.

A warm handshake from Dr. Aaronson and a kindly pat on the shoulder as a nurse led Andrew away to be X-rayed.

For the chest X-ray the day before, or was it a lifetime ago, he only had to take off his shirt. Now he had to strip down to his underpants and put on one of those ridiculous, badly fitting, hospital gowns. The tie on it was quite useless and he had to hold the gown in the middle to stop it opening as he walked to the X-ray table. That was one of the oldest tricks in the book: taking the victim's belt away. Not so much to stop him from hanging himself, but to humiliate him by making him have hold his pants up all the time. The X-ray table was hard. He had to turn this way and that way, on his front, on his back, on his side. On a few occasions the technician had to gently shift Andrew's body to make sure it was correctly positioned over the X-ray plates. By the end of process, Andrew felt exhausted. And yet this was nothing compared with the manhandling that Suslov was going to experience.

When Andrew finally got home he was in a daze. As he tried to process, yet again, his meeting with Aaronson, he realized how glad he was that Aaronson hadn't asked him how he actually felt about the news. He hadn't a fucking clue, and if he had been asked he might have made a fool of himself, subjecting his doctor to an outburst of impotent rage at things beyond their control. Of course, he didn't know how he felt. It was just too much to deal with. Right now, the only thing he could deal with was to continue working on his play.

* * *

Second Interview at OGPU headquarters

Lieutenant M's office a few days after the first interview. As before, Suslov sits opposite Lieutenant M., and a guard stands by the door. A blind is pulled down over the window, and the only source of light is the desk lamp. Sitting in a corner behind the desk is another man. He's in the shadows. One can't see his face but one can make out that he's heavily built.

Lieutenant: Well comrade Suslov, it seems as though you didn't tell us the whole truth about what happened on the night of February 26th.

Suslov: How do you mean, comrade Lieutenant? I told you everything that happened that night. I went to the Lebedovskys' apartment to borrow a few lumps of sugar…

Lieutenant *(impatiently)*: I'm not interested in the sugar, comrade. I'm not interested in what you *did*. I'm interested in what you *know*.

Suslov: Know, comrade Lieutenant?

Lieutenant: Yes, comrade, *know*. Look at this list. *(Hands Suslov a sheet of paper.)* What do you see?

Suslov: It's a list of names…a long list. One, two, three… there must be over twenty names on it.

Lieutenant: Twenty-three to be precise.

Suslov: Who are they?

Lieutenant: They were all at the Lebedovskys' apartment on the night of February 26th. The night you went there to get some sugar, or so you claim.

Suslov: That's not possible, comrade Lieutenant. It's not possible that there were twenty-three people in the Lebedovskys' apartment.

Lieutenant: Why not?

Suslov: Their apartment is far too small to hold so many people. They only have two rooms and one of them has been partitioned to make an extra room for Ludmila Vasilevna's mother.

Lieutenant: But how would you know that, comrade? I thought you didn't know the Lebedovskys. But now it appears you know all the details of their living arrangements. Maybe you live there, too?

Suslov: No, comrade Lieutenant, I don't know the Lebedovskys. I don't know them at all. I only know about their rooms because a few months ago I helped Ludmila Vasilevna carry some parcels into her apartment, and she asked me to put them behind her mother's partition.

Lieutenant: Have another look at the list comrade. Do you recognize any of the names?

Suslov (*making a show of studying the list carefully*): Hmm... no, no...yes...Androv and Golubev...they live in our building, but the rest of the names I don't know.

The heavy-set man gets up from his chair, walks over to the desk and slaps a photograph on the desk in front of Suslov. The man then returns to his seat. He doesn't say a word.

Lieutenant: Do you recognize the man in the photograph? Was he at the Lebedovskys' apartment on the night of February 26th?

Suslov: I don't recognize him. When I went to borrow the sugar, I didn't look in the room where their guests were sitting. Should I know him?

Lieutenant: Enough of your sugar, comrade. His name is Osip Emilyevich Mandelstam. Do you know who he is?

Suslov: He's a poet, isn't he?

Lieutenant: So you read his work, do you?

Suslov: No, I don't. I'm not big on poetry. I'm more interested in music. One of my colleagues at the institute likes poetry. He may have told me about this Osip Emilyevich. But I haven't read him myself.

Lieutenant: And the name of your colleague is...never mind, we can always find that out later. Osip Emilyevich is indeed a poet. Some say he's a good poet, but I wouldn't know about that. What I do know is that he's a dangerous poet, a subversive poet, an enemy-of-the-people poet, a poet who dares to criticize our great leader, Stalin. And, as you will be able to help us prove, comrade, he was at the Lebedovskys' apartment on the night of February 26th where he read a most subversive poem. A poem that made their twenty-three guests laugh, as you yourself told me. People who laugh at such poems are a danger to the State, a danger to us all. We must find them and help them see the error of their ways, don't you think?

Suslov *(very nervous)*: I, I...

Lieutenant: Well, the thing is, Andrei Ivanovich, you now have a great opportunity to be a true patriot. All you have to do is help us prove that all those people on that list were at the Lebedovskys' apartment, and that they heard Mandelstam's poem. That's not too much to ask, is it? To help you revive your memory we're going to let you sit in a nice quiet room by yourself with the list. That'll give you the chance to study it without any distractions. I'm sure the events of February 26th will all come back to you, and you'll be able to place everyone on that list in the Lebedovsky apartment.

Suslov: Can I let my wife know that I might be late coming home tonight?

Lieutenant: I don't think there's any need for that. I'm sure you'll get home...eventually. How is your wife by the way?

Suslov: That's why I want to let her know, comrade Lieutenant. I don't want her to worry. She's a bit under the weather. She was recently reassigned from her administrative position at the Ministry to work in the canteen. She was told it was to increase efficiency. The hard work has left her feeling very tired.

Lieutenant: Nothing like hard work, comrade. And I'm sure she likes working in the canteen. After all, she enjoys kitchen gossip, gossiping about the price of eggs, doesn't she? *(To the guard)* Take comrade Suslov to Cell 17. Take his watch. We don't want him to be distracted by worrying about the time. And take his belt, too.

(To Suslov) I'll come and visit you in a few hours to see if your memory has improved.

* * *

"It's a pleasure to meet you, Mr. Wallace. I'm just so sorry it has to be under these circumstances."

"I really appreciate you fitting me into your schedule at such short notice, Dr. Rubin."

"Not at all. Let me show you your skeletal survey and I'll explain what's going on. How much do you know about multiple myeloma?"

"I've read everything I could find on the Internet since I saw Dr. Aaronson."

"Excellent."

There was nothing excellent about it. Bone lesions were everywhere and a vertebra in the middle of his spine had partially disintegrated. That explained the strange back pains Andrew had occasionally experienced for over a year. Minor pains he'd omitted to mention at his annual check-up the year before. And that was the thing: one had to tell them everything, every little detail, because they could find out every little detail about you, even if you didn't know them yourself. Who knows what little details Suslov had failed to mention.

The relatively good news was that there were a variety of treatments for the bone damage, similar to the ones used for treating osteoporosis. Minimal side effects, for the most part. Dr. Rubin recommended starting regular infusions as soon as possible.

And now the blood tests. A long printout of numbers; most of them were in black—numbers in the normal range, the numbers of a healthy individual. It was the numbers in red that mattered. Light chain protein counts: kappa, lambda, kappa-lambda ratio. The normal ratio should be around one. Andrew's ratio was sky-high. The disease was spreading very aggressively as indicated by the bone damage. It was only because he was such a healthy individual and in such good shape that the symptoms were only starting to show through now—those little aches and pains, and the fatigue that he'd been experiencing recently.

It was Dr. Rubin's considered opinion that a highly proactive approach was needed to stop the disease. As he listened to what that meant in practice, Andrew mused over the phrase "highly proactive". Wasn't that doctors' talk for beating the shit out of you? Certainly the OGPU was going to be highly proactive with Suslov. At some point, no doubt, they would literally beat the shit out of him, even if there wasn't any shit left in him. The proposal for beating the shit out of Andrew was an autologous bone-marrow transplant, the sort that used the patient's own hematopoietic stem cells. According to Dr. Rubin, the autologous transplants had a far higher survival rate than those requiring a donor. If successful, the transplant could give Andrew several years of remission.

Now there were more sinister turns of phrase to mull over: "minimal side-effects", "survival rate", "if successful". Andrew doubted if the OGPU would worry that much about minimal side effects on Suslov. At most, they might try to minimize the visible bruising from the first couple of beatings. As for a successful outcome, that would mean getting Suslov to sign off on the list of those twenty-three traitors who had dared to laugh at Stalin. After Suslov signed he might be shot or he might be let go—a broken man, a vassal of the state. But in truth, his survival was immaterial. It would probably depend on what mood the OGPU officer was in when Suslov signed his statement, or if there were any execution quotas that had to be filled that week.

Andrew juggled these thoughts about his play as he listened, as attentively as he could, to what the doctor was saying. It was a lot to take in. Any further questions? They could all be answered by the Nurse Practitioner who would now take over. What a relief, a calm, empathetic individual who walked him through everything he would be going through over the next few months—the rest of his life, really. She explained the road map: a couple of months of strong chemotherapy to stabilize the disease; the protocol for "harvesting" his stem cells; and the transplant itself—a very demanding procedure that would require up to two weeks in hospital in a tightly controlled environment. And then, if things went well, the long recovery process. Probably a year or so. Dr. Rubin had already explained much of this, but this second account from a gentler individual was easier to digest. A lot to think about: information packets to take home and read, papers to review and sign. Time to plan the domestic logistics needed for his recovery period. Time to get one's affairs in order.

And then there were all those new usages of language to consider. Harvesting: Stalin had harvested millions of kulaks, ruined years of grain harvests, and starved a nation. For Andrew, they were going to harvest millions of his stem cells to keep him alive. A highly controlled environment: that meant solitary confinement in a specially equipped hospital room designed to minimize the risk of infection. Suslov would be locked up in a cold, damp cell and have to sleep on a stone bunk. Papers to sign: all they wanted from Suslov was his signature on a false statement. Andrew's papers were his informed consent to the procedure, his understanding of the risks involved. Getting one's affairs in order: for Andrew that meant reviewing his will, setting up powers of attorney, having the conversation he didn't want to have with his daughter and ex-wife. What would Suslov have to plan for? Maybe getting his small, illegal horde of cash to a safe place before the OGPU ransacked his apartment. Telling his wife that he was sorry, truly sorry, for his affair with Golubev's wife and his other infidelities. That he was sorry for hitting her when he was drunk. That he was sorry for everything.

Andrew and Suslov were brothers now, but relatively speaking, even if he didn't make it, Andrew knew he was the lucky one.

The Nurse Practitioner wished him well and gave him a special phone number he could call at any time. He liked her. She told him that she had worked with Dr. Rubin for many years. Andrew was in the best possible hands. Maybe she said that to all the patients, but he believed her. He had to.

*   *   *

Cell 17 at OGPU headquarters.

The cell is completely bare except for a cement block bunk along one wall and a slop bucket in one corner. There's no window. The only light comes from a bulb hanging from the ceiling. Suslov is sitting on the bunk holding the list. He looks tired. The cell door opens. Lieutenant M. enters and stands over Suslov.

Lieutenant: Peaceful in here, isn't it, comrade…

Suslov: How long have I been here?

Lieutenant M. I couldn't say, comrade. How's your memory now? Do you recognize any more names on the list? You know, all those people you saw in the Lebedovskys' apartment.

Suslov: There is one more. Pinsky.

Lieutenant: So you know Boris Abramovich Pinsky, do you?

Suslov: I don't know him personally. But a couple of weeks ago I ran into Sergei Mikhailevich in our building entrance, and he was with a man whom he introduced to me as Pinsky.

Lieutenant: Why did he introduce you to Pinsky?

Suslov: I don't know, comrade Lieutenant.

Lieutenant: Was Pinsky at the party of subversives at the Lebedovskys' apartment on February 26th?

Suslov: I think I caught a glimpse of him as I was leaving.

Lieutenant: A glimpse? No more than a glimpse? But enough to say that he was definitely there?

Suslov: I think so. Yes.

Lieutenant: Excellent. But why only one more name, comrade? It's taken you such a long time sitting here all by yourself just to remember that one name. Think how long it'll take you to remember the remaining twenty. You could be here for another few days, if not longer, much longer. You know comrade, sometimes there are little mental exercises that can help one remember things. Let's take the number of sugar lumps you borrowed from the Lebedovskys on the night of February 26th. Can you remember the number? No? Well, I can remember for you. It was seven. One each for you and Maria Kirilovna for your evening tea, two each for your coffee the next morning, and the seventh lump was for the cup of tea Maria Kirilovna had before going to the shops later that day. That day being February 27th, of course, and February 27th being a Tuesday, and Tuesdays being the day your wife likes to go shopping. So, you see, it was seven lumps.

Suslov *(clearly defeated)*: Yes, comrade Lieutenant, it was seven lumps.

Lieutenant: I'm glad that worked, comrade. Let's do another little memory exercise. I'm sure you think of yourself as a family man, don't you. Yes? Good. Well, as a good family man, I'm sure you know how many cousins Maria Kirilovna's half-brother has in Kharkov. You don't? Well, it's four. There's a rumor that one of them might be involved in the black market there. That would be very bad if proved to be true, comrade. Black marketeers are true enemies of the state, and a black mark on their families, too. Black marketeers have to be stamped out ruthlessly. It's important to make an example of such social vermin, don't you think? I certainly hope it's a false rumor… *(The Lieutenant pauses for a few moments.)*

You know, comrade, I think you should go home now. Take a rest and refresh your memory. *(The Lieutenant knocks on the cell door. The door opens. Suslov stands up holding his pants.)*

Suslov: Thank you, comrade Lieutenant.

Lieutenant: Don't thank me, comrade. Thank your wife.

Suslov: My wife?

Lieutenant: Yes, she came here looking for you. We had a nice little chat. She told me about her reassignment to the Ministry canteen. I told her I would see if I could do something about that. Clearly all that gossiping about the price of eggs in the canteen kitchen has worn her out. Now off you go…and here's your belt and your watch. You won't want to be late for your appointment here tomorrow morning. Seven o'clock, sharp.

* * *

The meeting with Frank was completely predictable. He was devastated, absolutely devastated by the news. Indeed, most of the meeting was taken up with Frank demonstrating just how absolutely devastated he was. But as Andrew's agent, and friend, he would take care of everything and sort out the business with the movie scripts. And, of course, he would do anything, absolutely anything, to help. However, they should be optimistic and look to the future. Andrew should consider writing a memoir, or maybe even a one-man play, about his experiences as a cancer patient, as a cancer survivor. Frank could already see the publicity: famous playwright describes his journey through the valley of fear and the healing power of love. What fucking love, Frank? A guaranteed bestseller, promise me you'll think about it, Andrew. Fuck off, Frank.

The meeting to break the news to Natasha went better than Andrew had expected. Elaine insisted on being present—what a price to pay to regain a sense of family again, albeit temporarily. The most important thing for Natasha to understand was that he would be fine, absolutely fine. Lies, big and small, black and white, were the basic tools of his playwright's craft. But now they all needed to cling to the lies they had to believe in. Andrew felt it important to spell out the ground rules. No visits when he was in the hospital. In principle, they were allowed, but there were too many risks because his immune system would be badly compromised by the treatment. He would communicate with them from the hospital by email. No phone calls because the doctors and nurses would be in and out of his room all the time, and it wasn't as though he'd have much to talk about. It was very sweet of both of them to volunteer to take care of him after he got home from the hospital. Although he was required to have help on hand, 24/7, for the first couple of weeks, he thought it'd be better to arrange for an agency nurse to live in. Dr. Rubin thought that was an excellent idea. And anyhow, he'd be even less fun to be around than he usually was. They all knew what a curmudgeon he could be when he was writing a play, and this was going to be a play like no other. But give him a few weeks, and short visits would be very welcome. Maybe after a few months they could all go on a short vacation. Nothing fancy. They could stay in Frank's beach house outside Santa Barbara for a few days. Some walks along the beach together would do him good, would do them all good. By the end of the family conference Andrew saw in Natasha's eyes that he was no longer the famous and remote dad. He was just an ordinary dad now, a vulnerable dad, a dad who needed his daughter. He was, at last, a loveable dad. He had no idea what Elaine felt. But then, he never really did.

Actually, he had told them a pack of little lies. All those ground rules were of his own making. They differed from the recommendations in the information packets he'd been given. They emphasized the importance of staying connected with family and close friends, of not becoming too isolated. Brief visits at the hospital from loved ones were a good idea. Having a friend or family member, suitably briefed, as the caregiver at home was also recommended. He'd never discussed using an agency nurse with Dr. Rubin. Family and friends, love and support, were all an important part of the recovery process. But Andrew felt differently. He knew he'd want to be left alone. Some of that was sheer vanity.

He'd feel like crap and look like crap. He wouldn't want to look at himself, let alone let other people see him—least of all his daughter who would insist on FaceTime if they spoke on the phone. It was just the way he was. Writers were solitary beasts.

How would Suslov fare? What chances would he have to enjoy the love and support of family and friends? None. Would Maria Kirilovna go to the Big House every day trying to find out information about him? Would she, along with all those other wives, try to bribe a guard to give her husband a note or a couple of pieces of sugar? If Suslov was lucky enough to survive his interrogations and be exiled to the middle of nowhere for ten years, would Maria Kirilovna follow him? Andrew doubted it. She'd probably had enough of his drinking and infidelities.

*   *   *

OGPU headquarters, Cell 17.

Suslov is sitting on the bunk. The cell door opens and the heavy-set man who had shown Suslov the photo in the Lieutenant M's office walks in.

Suslov: I thought I was going to have another meeting with Lieutenant M. today.

Heavy-set man: He's too busy to see you. You've been wasting far too much of his valuable time, you and your hopeless memory. Do you remember any more names on the list?

Suslov: Yes, there was another one. Karatov.

Heavy-set man: One more is not enough, comrade. The Lieutenant needs you to sign off on the whole list today.

Suslov: But I don't think I can.

Heavy-set man: Stand up.

Suslov stands up and the heavy-set man punches him hard in the stomach. Suslov collapses to the floor.

Heavy-set man: What are you doing on the floor? I told you to stand up.

Suslov struggles to his feet and the heavy-set man punches him again in the stomach, and Suslov collapses to the floor again. This cycle keeps on being repeated as the stage lights dim out.

*   *   *

Andrew was now spending most of his time at the Cancer Clinic undergoing a multitude of tests and treatments in preparation for his transplant. He had a port inserted in his chest. Suddenly he was quasi-bionic Andrew with a couple of tubes sticking out of his body so he could be hooked up to bags of this and bags of that. There was no pretending now that he wasn't a cancer patient.

Most of the time he sat in a room configured for four patients. In each corner there was a big recliner for the patient, a chair for a companion, and a workstation consisting of a computer and the equipment for administering intravenous drugs. Most of his fellow patients came with someone, usually a spouse or a friend. They would sit there quietly, often playing with their phones or tablets while the patient tried to snooze their way through their treatment. There would be the occasional jokey exchange with the nurses. Andrew went by himself. He would take his laptop, headphones to block out the chatter, and try to do some work. But he was usually too distracted to get much done. Sometimes he would eavesdrop on the conversations around him. One was absolutely remarkable. It could have been a scene in a play.

* * *

Cancer Clinic scene

A Norman Rockwell type couple in their early seventies. The man is lying back in the recliner. He's wearing a facemask and a John Deere cap is pulled down over his eyes. His wife is sitting next to him, and next to her is a nurse with whom she's chatting.

Nurse *(to man)*: We were quite worried about you last year, Mr. Edwards. It's great to see you again. You're quite the survivor, aren't you?

Mr. Edwards: *(makes a grunting sound).*

Mrs. Edwards *(to the nurse)*: Jim's a great survivor, you know. He survived a terrible car crash when he was in high school.

Mr. Edwards *(to no one in particular in a weak voice)*: And a helicopter crash.

Mrs. Edwards *(to the nurse)*: He was in Vietnam, you know. The worst of it.

Mr. Edwards *(to no one in particular)*: Eleven.

Nurse: Eleven?

Mr. Edwards: Yes. There were eleven of us, and four hundred of them. I thought it was time to kiss my ass goodbye… *(He then falls silent).*

Mrs. Edwards *(continuing the narrative)*: They called in the air force. They napalmed the whole area. It was just like that scene in the movie. I don't know how anyone survived. Jim told me all about it last year just before his big surgery. That was the first time he'd ever spoken about it.

*   *   *

Andrew estimated that Jim Edwards must have been a teenager at the time; just another kid pulled off the farm and thrown into the inferno. It didn't matter whether it was 400 Viet Cong or 40 Viet Cong, you'd be scared shitless. Andrew had never experienced anything remotely like that. In fact, he couldn't even imagine it. In principle, Suslov could have had some horrific experiences during the civil war, but that wasn't part of the play. After an experience like that, Andrew suspected that Jim Edwards wasn't going to be too scared of cancer. He wished he could have asked him that: whether he was less scared now than he was then. But that wasn't the sort of thing you could ask a stranger, even a fellow cancer patient. Perhaps it was something you couldn't even ask your closest friend, or even yourself. Andrew had the feeling that from now on, every time he heard the number eleven he'd think of Jim Edwards.

In addition to all the infusions, injections, and tests, there were meetings with various counselors. A psychological evaluation to determine if he could handle the emotional stress of what he was about to go through. So important to talk it all through with loved ones. One might also want to seek spiritual guidance and talk to a minister. One should definitely take advantage of all the support groups available: the groups for patients, for patients and caregivers together, and groups for the caregivers alone. Some patients attended the post-transplant support groups for a long time. There were also alternative therapies available to help relieve pain, nausea, stress, and anxiety. There was Acupuncture, Reflexology, Reiki, Tai Chi, Qi Gong, chair yoga, and a beading group. It was all a matter of doing whatever helped. Andrew said he would consider joining the beading group. Andrew recalled Groucho Marx's quip that he wouldn't join a club that would have him as a member. And now Andrew had joined a club that no one wanted to be a member of, even though it was club that went out of its way to help its members. No such club existed for Suslov. The only thing he might have was his circle of friends. And how many of them would be brave enough to stick with him once he'd been branded by the OGPU?

Objectively, Andrew was fascinated by everything he was being put through. He read everything he could find about the various treatments and procedures. Even if he didn't understand all the technicalities, it was clear that bone marrow transplants—the result of years of research and clinical trials—were a triumph of medical science. Andrew was particularly intrigued by the procedure used to harvest his stem cells. First, there was a series of daily injections to stimulate their production in his bone marrow. He'd been warned that he could experience some back pain, possibly quite a lot. And indeed he did. At a certain point, the pain was so excruciating he wondered if he should go to the emergency room. He called the special number Dr. Rubin's nurse had given him. She told him that it was a very good sign—an indication of intense bone marrow activity. He should try to hang in there as best he could and double the doses of pain medication. It was, she said, a case of the worse, the better. Andrew wished he could have laughed. The worse, the better! Trotsky would have been delighted to know that his revolutionary slogan still lived on for the advancement of medical science for the good of the masses, mobilizing millions of bloody foot soldiers on the cellular scale.

After a five-day course of injections, Andrew was plumbed into a machine through which his blood was circulated. It was a machine with an impressive array of dials and digital displays. It was difficult to imagine a more intimate relationship between man and machine. They were blood brothers in the most macabre sense. It was like something out of a Frankenstein movie. As his blood whirled through the machine it syphoned off his newly produced stem cells. The long and tiring process was repeated on two successive days. The precious harvest was then stored in the deep freeze until the transplant. The only machine Suslov might get hooked up to was one that administered electric shocks. It would be a machine with a single dial used to crank up the voltage, a voltage strong enough to fry a man alive.

D-Day. Andrew checked into the hospital and was shown to his room. Single occupancy with its own toilet and shower. He was told to change out of the clothes he'd arrived in, bag them, and change into some clean clothes, his pajamas if he liked. Everything he brought with him, his case, computer, phone, etc., was wiped down. Life of solitary confinement in the carefully controlled environment had begun.

Dr. Rubin walked him through the schedule. It was a military precision timetable of infusions, tests and monitoring. First, a strong dose of a cytotoxic drug, and then the infusion of his harvested stem cells back into his blood stream. The side effects of the drug would be a very sore throat, nausea, bad diarrhea, vomiting, feelings of extreme weakness. One couldn't pretend that it wasn't going to be a rough few days. He'd be permanently hooked up to an intravenous drip. But however rotten Andrew felt he should try to drink as much as possible and eat what he could, even if it didn't stay in very long. Scrupulous hygiene was essential and he had to shower every day using a special soap. If he felt too weak to shower by himself, the nurses could always help. Nurses would come in every hour, day and night, to monitor his vital signs. He wouldn't get much sleep. He'd probably lose track of time. He might even experience some hallucinations, although that was very unlikely. It was also important to keep moving, to stimulate his circulation. He should try and walk around the room as much as he could, and he was allowed to walk up and down the ward corridor, wearing a mask and wheeling his drip with him. Yes, it would be a challenge, but Dr. Rubin was very confident of Andrew's ability to handle it all. All would be well. He was confident of a successful outcome.

Andrew found himself in a twilight zone. Time was measured not by hours but by visits from the nurses and doctors, and by all-too-frequent trips to the toilet. The entire focus of a day, whatever day really meant, was his shower; a walk along the ward corridor; trying to eat half a banana and hoping it would stay in. He tried to watch television, but the images didn't register. He tried to read, but he couldn't absorb the words. He tried to listen to music, but the notes didn't sink in. He needed all his mental energy to look at his email. Natasha sent him jokey emails. Should she order him a large pizza with extra pepperoni and jalapenos? It took him the greatest effort to compose even the shortest replies and even more effort to make them sound cheerful. He fabricated tales of what he'd been reading and watching on TV, and what hospital delicacies he'd been eating. Lots of little white lies that no one would believe.

He couldn't find the words to describe how he felt. The man of words was at a loss for words. All he knew was that he felt as though he had absolutely nothing left. Characters in plays, including his own, would sometimes profess to feeling dead. Maybe this was how it really felt. He was glad nobody came to visit him. He wondered how Suslov was doing.

* * *

Prison cell scene

A dark room looking like Cell 17, but now with two stone bunks on opposite walls. There is a man lying on each bunk: Andrew Wallace and Andrei Ivanovich Suslov.

Andrew: You must be Andrei Ivanovich.

Andrei: Do we know each other, comrade?

Andrew: Yes. We do.

Andrei: It's difficult to know who anybody really is these days, but I'll take your word for it. What are you in for?

Andrew: A genetic mutation.

Andrei: A common crime these days. I'm in for poetry.

Andrew: Poetry? How's that?

Andrei: The usual story. I was accused of hearing something I wasn't supposed to hear. It was at a party at my neighbor's apartment. A party I wasn't even invited to. They wanted to know everyone who was there. They said Mandelstam had been there, reading a banned poem. A subversive poem. A poem that would incite leftist deviationism, or was it petty bourgeois revisionism? I can't remember which one. But it doesn't matter which one, they'll always find a crime to fit the case.

Andrew: Was Mandelstam there?

Andrei: No. It was a friend of his who recited the poem, from memory. Nobody would risk having a written version. To think, comrade, that great Russian tradition of reciting poetry is now a crime. Even listening to poetry is a crime. These days, poetry can get you shot. Who'd have thought it?

Andrew: But why did they pick on you? Why you, Andrei? It doesn't seem fair. You weren't even invited to the party. How did they know about it and the poetry reading?

Andrei: I think it was my wife, Maria Kirilovna. I think she betrayed me.

Andrew: Why would she do that?

Andrei: She was mad at me because I was having an affair with Golubev's wife. She knew about my other affairs, but she couldn't stand it when it was with someone living in the same building. My little Masha was cunning. She liked to gossip with Ludmila Lebedovskaya in the communal kitchen. When she heard there was to be a party at the Lebedovkys' apartment and Mandelstam might be there to read some of his poetry, she sent me there to ask for some sugar. And, of course, I stayed and heard the poem. The terrible thing was that in hatching her little plot, Masha not only took me down but everyone else who was there. She was so angry with me that she didn't care who else got hurt in the process. She even contrived a little ruse with the OGPU to avoid me being suspicious of her. They made it look as though she had been demoted at work because of me. But I worked it all out in the end. My wife betrayed me and now they want me to betray a bunch of people I don't know.

Andrew: Will you? Will you betray them?

Andrei: It won't make any difference if I do or I don't. They'll get all of them, either way. They always do.

Andrew: And how are you feeling right now, Andrei? If you don't mind me saying so, you look like crap.

Andrei: Couldn't have put it better myself, comrade. I'm so tired. They barge into my cell all the time and shine torches in my eyes to make sure I don't get any sleep. Beat me up when they feel like it. And they feed me garbage, I think it really is garbage, to make me sick. I throw up all the time and have the runs. And how are you doing, comrade?

Andrew: Exactly the same as you. They deprive me of sleep and feed me poison, but they say it's all to do me good.

Andrei: You know, comrade, I'm thinking about giving up. I don't think there's any point in going on. The only thing that keeps me going is to show them that they can't defeat me as easily as they'd like. What about you?

Andrew: Good question, Andrei, I just don't know. I just don't know.

*   *   *

And then, somehow, it was over. Everything had gone very well. Andrew had recovered from the transplant procedure ahead of schedule, and Dr. Rubin said he could go home. It had been eleven days.

During the next three months Andrew learned the true meaning of "one day at a time." Step-by-step progress. Being able to eat and taste a little more; being able to walk a little further; being able to concentrate a little longer; being able to complete trivial domestic tasks; being able to make a trip to the store without feeling wiped out for the rest of the day. There were frequent visits to the Cancer Clinic to monitor his recovery. It was nice to see the clinic nurses again. He liked to think they were pleased to see him again, too.

He had a visit from Frank, a visit from Elaine and several visits from Natasha. He promised her that as soon as he could, they would go out for pizza, just the two of them. It now seemed like the most important thing in the world he could do. He couldn't wait.

It was now time for Andrew's 100-day evaluation. Dr. Rubin was very pleased, some of the best recovery results he'd seen. They had a long talk about the side effects of the treatment. Andrew had lost his sense of taste. It seemed to be coming back, but many things still had a metallic taste. Would his taste buds ever return to being completely normal? Andrew's hair had grown back quite quickly, but he'd noticed that it now looked darker, a little less grey. No complaints there! And there was still the fatigue and reduced powers of concentration. He was trying to get back to work on the play he'd started before the diagnosis.

Dr. Rubin was in a cheerful and expansive mood, happy to talk, man to man, with another professional at the top of his field. Yes, a loss of taste was quite common but it usually returned. Hair re-growth could go many different ways: thinner, thicker, straighter, curlier, lighter, darker. Every patient was different. It was impossible to predict. Fatigue was quite normal. It was important to exercise as much as possible. Gentle exercise, of course: short walks and the like, but no swimming in a public pool for a year. He was sure Andrew's powers of concentration would return. Patients of Andrew's intellect tended to be more conscious of these things. Nothing to worry about. He'd just like to see Andrew gain some more weight.

During this discussion there was a curious moment. In fact, to Andrew's ears—so attuned to the choice and meaning of words—it was a stunning moment. In describing how difficult it was to predict how any one patient might react to a given treatment, Dr. Rubin commented that this was especially so for extreme procedures like a bone marrow transplant when the treatment involved sub-lethal doses of cytotoxic drugs. In the hospital, Dr. Rubin had used the term "strong dose" but apparently that was just a euphemism. It was a sub-lethal dose. Surely that was a term that shouldn't be used in front of patients? It must have slipped out. But there it was: *sub-lethal*. That was it, the key to the whole experience, the whole play.

Although Andrew understood the working principles of his bone-marrow transplant, the word sub-lethal was revelatory. It distilled the whole thing down to its barest, most brutal, essence. So they really did try to kill you. Or rather, almost kill you. Kill you just enough to kill off as many cancer cells as possible and then, if all went according to plan, or was it luck—probably a bit of both—you came back from the dead. Indeed, that was exactly how he'd felt in the hospital. Now he understood why. The interesting question was whether Suslov would also be at the receiving end of sub-lethal treatment. They would happily beat Suslov to within an inch of his life, but just keep him alive just long enough to sign his confession. But unlike Andrew, for whom every technique of modern medicine was used to help him return from the dead, nobody would give a shit about Suslov. He'd be left on the brink. Maybe he'd come back, maybe not. Or maybe he'd be kicked over the edge to make room in Cell 17 for the next victim. The OGPU had to be efficient. It had to fulfill its quotas.

More importantly, Andrew now saw what his own problem was. Although he was making an excellent physical recovery, he was still shot mentally. And the problem was his play. It was no longer a play about Suslov. It had become a play about Andrew and Suslov. The patient was becoming the victim and the victim was becoming the patient. The play kept on sucking him back into that hospital room, and into Suslov's cell. The play wasn't giving him the chance to start thinking clearly about what lay ahead in his new, reconstructed life. In Andrew's opinion, any play that was too much about the playwright was doomed to failure. It was clear what had to be done. Suslov had to be killed off, unceremoniously kicked over the edge into that vast pit filled with all of Stalin's other victims. Andrew also needed to kill off Lieutenant M. and the thug who'd beaten Suslov to a pulp. It would be a case of executing the executioners. That was easily done—it happened all the time during Stalin's reign of terror. In fact, it was time to kill off the whole damned play and everyone in it: the Lebedovskys, the treacherous Maria Kirilovna, Golubev, Androv, Pinsky, and Karatov. That still left the remaining nineteen names on the OGPU list. Names no one knew, not even the playwright; but that didn't matter—most victims were nameless. And Andrew, as the playwright, could kill off anyone and anything he wanted, just like the Great Leader himself.

A year after the physical that had revealed his cancer, Andrew was back in Dr. Aaronson's office for an annual check-up.

"Andrew, you look great. I can see why Dr. Rubin's so pleased with your progress. It's difficult to believe that it's been a year. How are you feeling?"

How are you feeling? Such a good question. A question Andrew would never know how to answer anymore.

"I'm feeling well, thank you."

"Are you back at work full-time? I remember you telling me about a play you were working on last year. Have you been able to finish it?"

"No. I decided to drop it."

"May I ask why? It sounded so interesting."

"That was the problem, it became too interesting, far too interesting for its own good. So I killed it. Playwright's prerogative."

CPSIA information can be obtained
at www.ICGtesting.com
Printed in the USA
JSHW021834050223
37226JS00001B/6